Accident Prone

The death of Muriel Fayne in her house near Colombury in the English Cotswolds sets off a curious chain of events, mainly affecting her daughter Helen. A tiresome fall, a bolting horse, a possible poisoning, a car crash with which drugs may be associated—do these and other incidents merely suggest that Helen is becoming accident prone, possibly because she drinks a little too much, or are more sinister motives and forces at work?

The whole of Muriel's family, the local vicar, a man who would once have been known as the 'squire'—all are involved, as well as the Drayton Galleries, a nearby riding stables and Coriston College.

Eventually, Dr Band takes a hand in the game, and so does Detective-Superintendent George Thorne of the Thames Valley Police Serious Crime Squad, as incident follows incident in this complex web of motives and deceptions, leading to a denouement as surprising as it is dramatic.

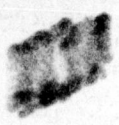

by the same author

JOHN PENN

Accident Prone

THE CRIME CLUB

COLLINS, 8 GRAFTON STREET, LONDON W1

William Collins Sons & Co. Ltd
London · Glasgow · Sydney · Auckland
Toronto · Johannesburg

First published in the UK 1987
© 1987 by John Penn

British Library Cataloguing in Publication Data

Penn, John
    Accident prone.—(Crime Club)
    I. Title
    823'.914[F]   PR6066.E496

ISBN 0 00 232145 9   -386-

Photoset in Linotron Baskerville by
Rowland Phototypesetting Ltd
Bury St Edmunds, Suffolk
Printed in Great Britain by
William Collins Sons & Co. Ltd, Glasgow

CHAPTER 1

South Winds was quite a small house, not built of Cotswold stone and certainly not a Cotswold mansion, though its rooms were well-proportioned. One of its main attractions lay in its spacious garden, and a second useful feature was its relative seclusion. The property lay in a kind of enclave at the far end of the extensive grounds of a true mansion, known locally in the village of Windfield as the Hall. A nineteenth-century owner of the Hall, in a moment of stupidity or financial embarrassment, had sold the freehold of the plot to a farmer and eventually South Winds had been built on it.

It was a perfect day in July, and Muriel Fayne, the present owner of South Winds, sat by her open french windows and looked out at her sunlit garden. The sky was a pale blue, fluffy white clouds moved lazily, and a gentle breeze carried the scent of roses into the sitting-room. But Muriel sighed irritably. In the distance she could hear the phut-phut of tennis balls, laughter and the splashing of water from her neighbours' swimming pool; clearly the Clutton-Greys, who now owned the Hall, were having a house party, and the sounds of cheerful activity were at the root of Muriel's irritation.

Other people's activity always annoyed her nowadays; she was becoming less tolerant as she grew older. Slowly and carefully Muriel pushed herself out of her chair. She leant firmly on her stick and moved with difficulty as she negotiated the step over the edge of the french windows down on to the patio. Muriel Fayne was a tall, heavy woman, five feet ten in height and big-boned, and it was due to her build, at least in part, that the surgery on her hips had not been successful. And now, at just over eighty, her arthritis had almost crippled her. This she resented bitterly, especially on a beautiful July day.

When she was young, she had walked for miles, played tennis and golf, swum in the sea when the family went on holiday and danced whenever she got the chance. She had been a pretty girl, fair-haired and blue-eyed with a creamy skin—a typical English rose, and always in demand. Marriage, a World War and two small daughters had naturally changed her life, but the biggest change had come some twenty years ago.

As she advanced, step by careful step, across the lawn to the seat beside the lily-pond, Muriel Fayne recalled that period with bitterness. She was fully aware of the nature of her chronic complaint, but other people, seemingly no matter what their age, had their hip-joints replaced, and rejoiced in their rejuvenation. For her, however, the result of surgery had been disastrous; in the space of a few weeks she had become a semi-invalid—and the best medical advice was that nothing more could be done.

Then Colin, her husband, had been found slumped over his desk in his architect's office in Oxford. It seemed he had suffered a massive coronary, and collapsed before he could call for help. His death had been completely unexpected. He had rarely suffered even minor illnesses, and certainly there had been no hint of heart trouble. But the result was that Muriel had been left alone at a time when physically she was incapable of coping. What was more, Colin's business hadn't been doing too well and his resources were stretched, so there wasn't as much money as she might have liked.

Of course the situation could have been much worse. She still had the house, South Winds. She had an income that many widows would have envied and her married daughter, Bridget, lived nearby with her husband and children. But that didn't solve the problem of how she was to be looked after. Even if she could have afforded it she wouldn't have welcomed any kind of housekeeper or nurse or companion. All her life she had been cared for with an affection such as no paid help could provide.

To her friends and acquaintances the answer was obvious: Muriel Fayne must go to live with Bridget. Granted, Biddy had three young children, but she also had a large house and a good-natured husband, Paul Drayton, who had inherited enough capital to provide a comfortable income; this, incidentally, was fortunate, for the fact that Paul's business acumen was slight had become apparent almost as soon as he had opened the Drayton Galleries in the small market town of Colombury nearby. The whole thing would be a most suitable arrangement, the friends and acquaintances agreed, and it had the added advantage that Muriel could stay in a neighbourhood where she had lived for many years and was well-known and well-liked.

To Muriel, however, the answer was not so obvious. She loved Biddy, who was tall and fair and resembled Muriel as she had been in her youth, and she tolerated Paul, but she had no intention of living with them and their noisy children. She refused to give up her own house and her independence, to become, eventually and inevitably, an unwelcome addition to a happy family.

Muriel resolved the problem in her own way. If she wouldn't live with Biddy, Helen should come to live with her. That her elder daughter had an excellent job in London and might have little desire to return to the Cotswolds didn't affect the issue. Helen was unmarried and, with her sharp tongue and unattractive appearance, in her mother's opinion likely to remain so. Her small flat was only leased and sub-letting should present no difficulty. As for her work, the quality of which Muriel was inclined to underrate, Helen could use her skill as an interior decorator helping her brother-in-law in his gallery.

And it had all worked out splendidly, Muriel thought as, her irritation forgotten, she leant on her stick by the edge of the lily-pond and gazed around the garden with satisfaction. She had no doubts. She couldn't have made a better decision, for herself, for Biddy, for the Draytons—and for Helen. Whatever Helen might have felt twenty years ago at her mother's peremptory summons, her return home had been well-rewarded. She had a house where she could give adequate rein to her natural domestic instincts; she liked to cook and sew and garden. She had family and friends. Most especially, she had work she enjoyed; it was she who had made a success of the Drayton Galleries—something that poor Paul could never have achieved alone. In doing so, she had earned respect in the neighbourhood and indeed throughout the Cotswolds.

Muriel Fayne's smile of contentment faded, to be replaced by a grimace of pain. She had thought she heard a sound in the house behind her—she was expecting the vicar, the Reverend Timothy Merle, for tea—and had turned too quickly, sending a ripple of agony through her body. She gritted her teeth and closed her eyes. She was never to know exactly what happened next.

She felt her stick cease to support her. She opened her eyes and cried out. She was aware of someone near her. There was a soft blow between her shoulder-blades—or had she imagined it? In any case, she was falling. She flung out her arms in an attempt to save herself, but it was useless. She fell forwards into the pond. Her face was enveloped in a lily-pad and her fingers seized on its long, dangling root as if she believed the fragile plant would bear her weight.

The water in the lily-pond was not deep. A child might have drowned in it, but Helen Fayne had created it only after her niece and nephews had become teenagers. And any adult falling in should have been able to scramble out with ease. But Muriel was old, heavy and infirm. She thrashed about, momentarily in a panic. She swallowed water, mud that had sifted up from the bottom, a minute piece of gravel. She choked. Somehow she knew that she was going to die, pathetically, ignominiously—not in a way she had pictured. The thought angered her momentarily and she tried to force herself to be calm. Almost at once she felt helping hands trying to lift her from the pool.

Then she realized with horror that the hands were not helping her; on the contrary, they had taken her by the shoulders and were holding her down. She began to struggle again, but now it was too late and she no longer had the heart or strength to put up a real fight. Her body went slack, and her thoughts drifted away to the time when she was young and pretty and loved. Soon she was dead. But it was five minutes before the hands released her, their owner confident that, should someone interrupt, the scene could be interpreted as an attempt at rescue rather than a successful killing.

The Reverend Timothy Merle came out of his cottage next to the church of St Augustine at the end of the village of Windfield, and mounted his bicycle. It was an old and battered machine, and his stately progress on it was such as to induce occasional laughter from strangers; if this happened, the Reverend Timothy merely raised his hat—a panama in summer, a deer-stalker in winter—and wished them good day. In the village and the district he was a well-known figure, and generally appreciated, though, except at weddings and funerals, the congregation of the Norman church he served rarely numbered more than a few dozen.

On this particular afternoon he stopped at the village store-cum-post office to buy some stamps and chatted to Mrs Beale, the postmistress, and Mrs Ferguson, one of her customers, until he suddenly remembered the time.

'Four o'clock,' he said. 'Oh dear, I shall be late. I'm due at South Winds for tea.'

Mrs Beale exchanged glances with Mrs Ferguson, who 'helped out' at the Faynes' on three mornings each week. The vicar's frequent visits to South Winds were a favourite topic of conversation between them. Timothy Merle, with his thin body and spindly legs, always looked half-starved, and they suspected, giggling, that one of Helen's main attractions for him was the excellent food she provided.

Fortunately the Reverend Timothy had no idea of these speculations. He got back on his bicycle and pedalled quickly out of the village, soon to turn right towards South Winds. His long, pale face began to sweat, and with a finger he loosened his dog-collar. He wished he felt less nervous.

He reached the house at eight minutes past four, leant his cycle against the wall and rang the doorbell sharply three times. He expected no answer; his ring was merely a polite and routine warning to Mrs Fayne that he had arrived, and was waiting for a moment before letting himself into the house.

He called, 'It's me, Mrs Fayne. Tim Merle.'

He glanced into the sitting-room, which ran from front to back of the house, then went along to the kitchen. His mouth watered as he guiltily lifted the cloth that covered the tea-trolley and inspected the food that Helen Fayne had prepared—sandwiches, scones, two kinds of cake and biscuits. He had had nothing to eat since breakfast—porridge and a piece of toast; there was a good deal of truth in the gossips' suspicions that he was half-starved.

Hurriedly he replaced the cloth—he thought he heard a noise outside—and went to the window, which overlooked the back garden. He stared, frowning. There was a strange shape in the lily-pond, blue and billowing as the breeze moved it.

He knew what it was, and he knew what he must do. Bile

rose in his throat as he let himself out of the back door and ran down the garden to the pond. Regardless of his shoes and his best trousers, he plunged into the water. He clutched Muriel's body under the armpits and pulling, struggling, once slipping so that he too was immersed, he managed after several attempts to move her on to the grass.

For a moment, he gasped for breath. Then he knelt beside Muriel Fayne and forced himself to search for a pulse in her wrist and at her neck. Reluctantly, he put his ear to her ample bosom. Then, covering his face with his hands, he prayed silently. Eventually he decided he must straighten her disarranged blue dress so that she was decent.

Finally, Merle stood up and looked at his watch. It was twenty-five minutes past four. He didn't know whether or not to be surprised that so little time had elapsed since he had left the company of Mrs Beale and Mrs Ferguson at the post office.

He went into the house, and his wet clothes made a puddle on the hall carpet as he dialled Dr Band's number. Band, he knew, was the Faynes' doctor, and in any case his practice was the only one in the immediate area.

Dick Band answered the phone himself. He was in the middle of conducting his surgery in Colombury and sounded brusque. 'You're sure she's dead?' he asked.

'Yes. I've seen a—a drowned person before.'

'What have you done?'

'Done?'

'Artificial respiration? Kiss of life?' The doctor was impatient.

'No. Nothing like that. I—I made sure she was dead, that's all.'

'Very well. I'll be with you as soon as I can. Meanwhile, find something to cover her. A blanket, a rug—anything. Nurse Whittaker lives in the village. I'll try to get hold of her and send her along. Have you phoned anyone else? Mrs Fayne's family? The police?'

'No. Neither. There's not been time to call Miss Fayne and I never thought of the police. It was an accident. It must have been.'

'The police still have to be notified. But leave it, Mr Merle. Just cover her and wait till someone arrives. I'll deal with everything.'

'Yes. All right, Doctor. Thank you.'

Timothy Merle shivered. Normally Dick Band was a kind and friendly soul, and Merle failed to understand why on this occasion he had been so abrupt. He couldn't suspect— Surely Band couldn't suspect—

The vicar collected a blanket from Mrs Fayne's bedroom —he knew which was hers, as he had visited her when she was ill. He took it into the garden and, averting his eyes, wrapped it around the body. Then he returned to the house and washed his hands for at least two minutes before he put on the kettle to make himself some strong sweet tea; he knew what he needed if he were to cope adequately with the doctor and the police and the Fayne family and all the questions they would ask.

And fifteen minutes later when Nurse Whittaker bustled into the house, she found the Reverend Timothy Merle sitting at the kitchen table drinking tea and, to judge from what remained, making a meal of sandwiches and scones and cake.

CHAPTER 2

The Drayton Galleries were situated in Colombury, just off the High Street. The location, in a street much frequented by visitors to the picturesque Cotswold town, was good from the point of view of retail trade, but it was only since Helen's advent that the Galleries had begun to prosper—and in recent years they had done so beyond all expectations.

Originally the shop had been small, and bought by Paul Drayton's father so that his son, who was thought to have artistic inclinations but little likelihood of obtaining other qualifications, should have at least some sort of business of his own. In fact, at first the enterprise had been treated almost as a hobby. Later, as rates and overheads increased, Paul had faced a growing struggle to keep its losses to a minimum.

On her return to Oxfordshire, Helen had revolutionized the operation. She had cast a beady eye over the existing stock, discarded much of it and bought carefully, making use of her London contacts for advice—and in some cases for credit. She had examined the finances of the enterprise, made friends with the bank manager and persuaded Paul at first to rent, then to buy, the shops on either side. The three establishments were then knocked into one spacious area, with a gallery running around its perimeter. The effect was no longer old-fashioned and pokey, but stylish, spacious and airy. She herself had been responsible for the interior design, and for a good deal of the actual work, and she had efficiently supervised what she couldn't do personally.

The upstairs gallery, quite high above the ground floor and reached by a wide spiral staircase, was reserved for works of art—paintings and sculpture mainly by local artists, together with a selection of carefully-chosen and carefully-priced prints and casts by artists of international renown—while the ground floor served as a showroom for ceramics, china and glass, ornaments, local crafts and— in locked glass cases—some reasonably valuable modern jewellery. And, though the place was not in any sense a Cotswold 'antique' shop, Helen did on occasion buy wisely at local sales, and often resold the results of her bidding to special customers at a profit.

Biddy had at first objected to the amount of money that was being ploughed into the business, but for once Paul had failed to heed her comments. Soon the results were apparent to everyone. From a third-rate shop full of shoddy and often overpriced goods, the Drayton Galleries had become an elegant showroom. Moreover, since Helen knew how to advertise in the appropriate media and excite comment in influential circles, the fame of the Galleries gradually spread and visitors to the Cotswolds began to go out of their way to come to Colombury to visit them. In short, the Galleries became a most useful adjunct to the social and commercial life of the town, and Helen's own reputation grew with their success.

None of this was accomplished without a great deal of time and effort on Helen's part, and even when the Galleries had become a profitable concern she continued to work hard. Visits to potters, silversmiths, artists and sculptors, quite apart from auction sales, represented miles of driving, and even on her holidays she continued her labours, buying for the shop whenever opportunity offered, seeking new ideas for the interior decorating part of the business that she had begun to build up. After all, she maintained, if I can do the décor for a room, I can make sure it's filled with stock from the Galleries.

She had unbounded energy and she enjoyed her work. Nor had Muriel any cause for complaint. Helen ran their house with great competence, cooked, gardened and showed her mother every consideration. For this she had originally received nothing except free board and lodging, while her salary from the Galleries was moderate in the extreme. It was on her fiftieth birthday that, thinking of the future, she decided to do something about this situation.

Helen first tackled Paul. He was horrified at his previous

thoughtlessness, and immediately suggested that he and
Helen should become partners, splitting the profits equally.
Biddy, however, had protested that such a division was
over-generous. The original Galleries, bought by Paul's
father, belonged to the Draytons, she said, and this was the
basis of the business; true, Helen's contribution had been
massive, but this should be recognized by an increase in
salary, rather than by any partnership.

To Biddy's surprise their mother sided with Helen in
the ensuing negotiations, and eventually a more equitable
arrangement was reached. Helen was to use part of her
capital—increased by skilful investment of savings from her
salary as a senior employee in London—to buy a partnership, and the net income from the Galleries was to be shared
between her and Paul, in proportions to be decided upon
when the final figures were known. And, as if Muriel had
received a hint, she chose this moment to volunteer the
information that on her death Helen would inherit South
Winds. Helen, who was not a greedy woman, was more
than satisfied.

The Galleries continued to do well and, on the afternoon
that Muriel drowned in the lily-pond, business had been
particularly brisk. A party of Americans, on their way to
see *King Lear* at Stratford-on-Avon, had bought a collection
of small *objets d'art*. A local woman had chosen a table inlaid
with a chessboard as a birthday present for her lawyer
husband, and had been intrigued by some new linen table
napkins. To crown all, Sir Reginald Clutton-Grey, Muriel
Fayne's neighbour, had telephoned to say that he would
keep the painting of Colombury High Street that he had
had on approval for some time.

But when Mary Band, Dr Dick Band's wife, came into
the shop later in the afternoon, the showroom was empty,
and no one put in an appearance, in spite of the bell which
had rung to signal someone's arrival. Idly, Mary wandered

around. She hadn't come to buy anything, but to invite Helen, who was a friend, to supper the following week. After several minutes, while there was no sign of either Helen or Paul, she was about to leave, but decided first to try the office. She opened the door to the corridor that led to the office and the service entrance at the rear of the premises, and almost at once collided with Peter Drayton, Paul and Biddy's elder son.

'Oh! Mrs Band, hello! I—I thought I heard someone.'

'Hello, Peter. Where is everyone?'

'If you mean Dad and Aunt Helen, they're not here. Dad felt a bit queasy after lunch; it must have been something he ate. He went home a while ago. And Aunt Helen's gone off to the Slinters'. She's in the middle of a big interior decorating job for them.'

Peter Drayton spoke very fast. He smiled, but he didn't meet Mary Band's glance, and she wondered if he were lying, though she could imagine no reason why he should make up such stories. She told herself not to be fanciful. Give a dog a bad name, she thought, doing her best to be fair to the man.

But it was in fact difficult to have great faith in Peter Drayton. Like his father, he had left school early at sixteen with few qualifications—it was hinted that if he had not done so voluntarily he would have been expelled—and since then had drifted in and out of jobs, mostly out. On at least two occasions there had been minor trouble with the police, though no charges had ever been laid. Now, at thirty-two, a not unattractive wastrel, he lived at home, and helped at the Galleries erratically. As Helen had once confided to Mary Band, she was very fond of Peter, but she knew that no ordinary employer would put up with his timekeeping and general demeanour.

The bell in the shop rang, and Peter said, 'I must go. I'm meant to be holding the fort this afternoon.'

'You're not doing it too well,' Mary Band said a little tartly. 'I was in there for about five minutes alone. I could have walked off with anything.' She wished she had sounded less reproving. 'Didn't you hear the bell, Peter? It rang when I came in. I heard it.'

'Actually, no.' He moved past her quickly. 'Excuse me. This could be a valuable customer.'

Hardly tactful, thought Mary, to suggest that she herself was less than valuable. But in fact the newcomer was Helen Fayne. She looked flushed and angry. 'Those Slinters really are the limit,' she burst out to Peter. 'I'm sorry I ever agreed to do any work for them. First they want one thing, then they don't like it and want something else. And they don't pay as they promised.' She broke off as she caught sight of Mary Band. 'My dear, I'm sorry. How nice to see you! How's Dick?'

Before Mary could reply the telephone rang. Helen answered it. She put her hand over the mouthpiece. 'How funny, this *is* Dick! Someone—I didn't recognize the voice —said Dr Band wants to speak to me.'

She listened. 'Yes. Helen here. Yes.' And, after a pause. 'Of course, I'll come at once. Goodbye, Dick. And thank you.' She put down the receiver slowly and turned to Mary. She spoke without apparent emotion, her face expression-less. 'It's Mother. She's dead. Tim Merle found her drowned in the lily-pond when he arrived for tea. Poor man, it must have been a shock for him.'

'Poor Muriel!' Mary Band said, staring.

'I must go at once,' Helen said.

'Would you like me to come with you?' Mary asked.

'No, no. I'll be better on my own.' Helen turned and hastened from the shop before Mary could find further words.

Dick Band took off his dressing-gown and threw it over the back of a chair. Mary, already in bed, her latest library book open on her lap, regarded her husband dubiously. Something was worrying him, and it was not difficult to guess what. As far as she knew it had been a doctor's normal day, house calls in the morning—there was a mild virus going around—surgery in the afternoon. There had been but one untoward incident: Muriel Fayne's death. Admittedly the circumstances, as Dick had briefly retailed them to her over the dinner table, seemed to have been slightly bizarre, but surely not such as to give any cause for worry.

Mary turned a page as if she had been reading, and repeated what she had said at dinner. 'So sad about Muriel. So trivial, somehow. She'd have hated to die so trivially.'

'Yes.' It was a bare monosyllable.

Mary closed her book. 'Dick, what is it? What's the matter?'

'Who said anything was the matter?' But Dick grinned as he slipped into bed beside her. 'My dear, you're too perceptive for your own good, as usual. The fact is that, rightly or wrongly, I've got a nasty nagging doubt about the late Muriel Fayne.'

'What sort of doubt, for heaven's sake?'

'A doubt I'd best forget, because I haven't a hope of resolving it. It'll have to wait for the PM and the inquest.'

'Inquest?'

'Of course. You know perfectly well one's necessary in any case like this.'

'True,' said Mary. 'But, Dick Band, stop talking in riddles!' Mary pretended to be exasperated. 'There's no doubt it'll be a formality, is there? She fell into the lily-pond and drowned, didn't she?'

For a moment Band was silent as he visualized the scene —the pond, the broken lily-pads, the muddy trampled grass. Muriel Fayne had been heavy and arthritic, but she was strong. If she had slipped and fallen accidentally surely she should have been able to struggle out of what after all were only a few inches of water. There were no signs that she had hit her head. Even if she had felt giddy or faint, the sudden immersion in cold water could well have shocked her into consciousness. Band shrugged mentally. He was getting too suspicious; it came of being the local police surgeon, as well as a general practitioner.

Finally he said, 'No doubt, really. I'm being stupid. It's just that the Reverend Timothy Merle seems to have panicked. I can understand he had difficulty pulling her out of the pond, but I don't see why he had to wallow around in the water himself, destroying any evidence. Nor do I see why he didn't make at least some attempt at artificial respiration.'

'Evidence?' Mary Band was quick to seize on the word. 'Dick, what on earth do you mean? You're not suggesting someone pushed her in, are you?' She laughed aloud. 'Who would want to murder Muriel Fayne?' she demanded.

The doctor was prepared to laugh with his wife, but his laughter was less sincere. 'You never know,' he said eventually. 'There's always Helen, for example. She'll be free now, not tied to the old lady any more. She can do what she likes, go back to London if she wants.'

Mary shook her head, suddenly serious. 'She took the news of her mother's death rather oddly, I thought,' she said. 'But that must have been shock. It's too late for her,' she added positively. 'If it had happened ten years ago, it might have been possible, but not now. She's made her life here. She's wedded to the Galleries and the Draytons and their offspring. She's got friends all about, and she's involved in all sorts of local affairs. She's even got keen on horses and taken up hacking. No, I'm sure the idea won't even occur to her.'

Mary Band was wrong, though not completely so. The idea —or at least the realization of her new-found freedom—had occurred to Helen Fayne almost at once, certainly as soon as the initial confusion was over, and the police sergeant and his constable from the local station had inspected the scene with Dr Band. Later, the pathologist had arrived and examined Muriel, finally agreeing that the body could be removed to the mortuary in Oxford.

Yes, Helen had considered the impact of her changed circumstances. But she had borne her burden, such as it had turned out to be, for a long time now, and she was a practical woman. She knew that over the years new ties had been woven, new obligations undertaken and, for her own sake, she must make no radical changes in her way of life. Nevertheless, she couldn't constrain her feeling of excitement at the events of the afternoon and evening.

She found it hard to analyse this feeling, especially as it seemed to override any sorrow she might have felt at the loss of her mother. Her emotion worried her and kept her awake. She heard the grandfather clock in the hall strike one, then two. The acid indigestion from which she suffered chronically was troubling her, and she reached to the bedside table for the antacid tablets that Dr Band had prescribed for her, and which she took regularly, two or three at a time. The tablets eased her indigestion, but she still couldn't sleep.

Twenty minutes later, she got out of bed. She was reluctant to do so because, in spite of the strange mood in which she found herself, she felt tired, almost exhausted. Resignedly, she put on a robe and, a shapeless figure without her restraining girdle, went downstairs to the kitchen. A cup of tea might soothe her, prove a distraction, though it probably wouldn't help her to sleep.

She plugged in the kettle and, waiting for it to boil, wandered into the sitting-room. She opened the french windows, and gazed into the garden. The moon was nearly

full and the lily-pond might have been floodlit. Twenty-four
hours ago the view had been beautiful; now it was desolate.

The lily-flowers were scattered, their pads broken and
uprooted. The pond itself and the surrounding area had
been covered with tarpaulins by the police, but Helen knew
that underneath the grass around the pond was trampled
and covered with mud, the edge broken in a couple of places.
Now it looked what it had been, a scene of violence.

Helen sighed. She had loved the lily-pond. Even since she
had been a child and seen such a pond in a friend's garden
she had yearned to create one of her own. She had waited
until Peter and Gavin and Susan—the Draytons' three
children—were of responsible ages, and had then fulfilled
her ambition. Cynically, she wondered what her family and
friends would say if, after what had happened, she had it
repaired and restocked.

Biddy and Paul, she guessed, would be shocked; they
would probably consider it almost indecent. Gavin would
be indifferent but Peter, still her favourite nephew in spite
of his obvious irresponsibility, would tell her to go ahead,
to do as she pleased. Susan, who was married with a six-
year-old son, would certainly disapprove; she had already
begun insisting that the lily-pond was dangerous. Ironic,
Helen thought, that it should have been the elderly grandmother and not the infant grandson who had eventually
drowned there.

Smiling to herself, she shut the french windows and returned to the kitchen to make her tea. She sat at the table
to drink it, a short, square woman with a plain, heavy face,
but with intelligence far above the average. She wasn't
looking forward to the next week or so—she remembered
when her father had died—the post-mortem, probably an
inquest, the funeral, the inevitable assembly of the family
and the equally inevitable invitation to family and friends
to sherry after the ceremony.

Certainly the next week or so would be appalling, she thought. But after that . . .

CHAPTER 3

'. . . What has happened was unfortunate and tragic, but no blame for the event can be or should be attributed to anyone. Muriel Fayne had a good life. She was blessed with two devoted daughters. They loved her and cared for her into an old age, during which she bore her crippling arthritis bravely, stoically and with fortitude, like the splendid Christian she was. Her manner of death was, as I said, tragic but I repeat that no one can be blamed for this sad accident. Such unhappy events are—must be—the will of God. And we should all be grateful that He spared Muriel Fayne to live among us for so long.'

The Reverend Timothy Merle brought his eulogy to an abrupt close, and there was an audible sigh from the congregation—a gathering much larger than those to which the vicar was accustomed. The family was well-known in the district and, though Muriel Fayne had outlived many of her friends, people had come from some distance to pay their last respects.

In the front pew Helen Fayne, in a black suit that was too thick for the warm day and a straw hat that did nothing for her, had spent much of the time wondering how many of the congregation proposed to accept her purposely vague invitation to return to South Winds for drinks and a light buffet. Hoping that Mrs Ferguson and her helpers were dealing adequately with the food, and that there would be enough of it, she rose for the last hymn. Minutes later she felt the gentle pressure of her sister's hand on her arm, as a warning that it was time to follow the coffin down the aisle.

The two sisters went first behind the vicar, Biddy, attractive in grey and white, towering over Helen. Behind them came Paul Drayton, holding his grandson, Jeremy, by the hand. Susan followed, with her husband, Andrew Hill, and her two brothers, Peter and Gavin. Some distant cousins completed the family.

The congregation included Dr and Mrs Band. They had come to the funeral because Dick Band was the Faynes' family doctor and also, at Helen's firm request, to provide her with some moral support at the wake, as she called it. As they got into their car to drive to South Winds after the interment in the churchyard, Mary said, 'The Reverend Tim was a bit confused, wasn't he? I can understand his making the point about "God's will", but why the extraordinary emphasis on blaming no one? Why should anyone be blamed? After all, you told me that once the coroner had read the statements and got the PM report he said the inquest would be a mere formality. "Accidental death", surely.'

Band shrugged. 'You're quite right, of course. As for Merle, I don't know. I like him, but he's a strange fellow in many ways. I realize it can't have been pleasant to have to pull poor old Muriel out of the lily-pond, but he seems to have been disproportionately upset by the incident, especially as he claims he's seen at least one drowned corpse before.'

Mary was silent for a moment. Then: 'Maybe he feels guilty that he didn't arrive early—or on time—and save her.'

'Maybe. Or maybe he realizes he should have at least made an effort to revive her once he did get her out of the pond. But it's useless to speculate. The PM showed nothing unusual. She fell into that wretched pond and drowned. That seems to be clear enough. Why she wasn't able to get herself out again still remains something of a mystery, at any rate to me. However, no one else seems to be bothered about it, least of all the coroner, so it's best forgotten.'

Mary murmured her agreement. To change the subject as they neared South Winds, she said, 'There are the Slinters getting out of their car up ahead. I noticed them in church, but they weren't at the graveside. Surely they're not coming to the house. They've only just bought that big place of theirs. They can't have known Muriel Fayne, except very casually.'

'No. I doubt if they've ever been to South Winds. But they're clients of Helen's, aren't they? And they may be curious to see the famous lily-pond. If so, they'll be disappointed. It's all boarded up for the time being.' Dick Band rubbed his hand over his balding head as he brought the car to a halt. 'Strange how a violent—even an unexpected—death incites curiosity. I bet the Slinters won't be the only uninvited guests—if they weren't invited. There's quite a small crowd arriving.'

Mary Band regarded the people passing in twos and threes through the front door of South Winds. It was scarcely a crowd, but certainly there was a steady trickle. To her annoyance she realized that the Slinters—what on earth were their names? Frank and Jean, that was it—had seen them, and were waiting for them. She didn't particularly like them, but they were patients and one had to make an effort. She greeted them pleasantly.

'Hello. How are you?'

'No better for going to a funeral. I hate funerals. They always remind me of my own mortality,' Frank Slinter laughed loudly as he produced this cliché. He was in his late forties, a short, bluff, red-faced man whose shrewd blue eyes belied his apparent joviality. 'I'd hate to be in your line of business, Doc. You must see too much of death.'

'More than I like,' Band said shortly. He shared his wife's feelings about the Slinters, and he objected to being called 'doc', as if he were a character in an old American Western movie. He had also just remembered that Slinter, a private patient, who drove a Rolls and was reputed to have made a fortune out of property, hadn't yet paid his last bill, in spite of a reminder.

Jean Slinter said, 'We wouldn't have come today except for poor dear Helen's sake. She's a genius, you know. She's done absolute wonders with our house, made some marvellous suggestions. I can't imagine what I'd have done without her help.'

Wryly Mary recalled Helen's comments on the Slinters in the Galleries on the day Muriel died, but she smiled her acknowledgement of Mrs Slinter's remark, and thankfully took her husband's arm and went into the house. Biddy and Paul were on duty near the door of the sitting-room, shaking hands and accepting condolences. People stood around drinking sherry or wine, and talking. Voices, at first subdued, became louder as the inappropriate party atmosphere that always seemed inevitable on occasions such as this began to prevail. Mary could see no sign of Helen, and assumed that she was organizing food in the kitchen or dining-room.

Dick Band found himself standing beside Sir Reginald Clutton-Grey. 'Nice little house, this,' said Clutton-Grey suddenly, 'with quite a bit of garden. I've been trying to buy it, but the old girl was obstinate, though I kept on offering her twice the going price or more.'

The doctor knew that Clutton-Grey's estate almost surrounded South Winds, and thought he knew the answer to the obvious question. However, for want of anything else to say, he asked it: 'Why do you want it so much?' He was surprised by the vehemence of the response he received.

'Want it! Want it? I bloody well need it!' Clutton-Grey leant towards Band, so that Dick could smell the mixture of whisky, wine and tobacco that he exuded. Clutton-Grey was the sixth baronet, a Member of Parliament and a Justice of the Peace. He was thus a man of some importance, both locally and nationally, and he had intensely disliked being thwarted by Mrs Fayne.

He pulled himself together after his outburst, and glanced at the doctor. 'I more than need it,' he confided quietly. 'It's become essential. Between ourselves, it's like this. Mother would move here. She'd look on it as the dower house, and Kathleen would be happy with the arrangement. As it is . . .' He cast his eyes upwards. 'Women!' he exclaimed.

Dick Band was amused. He had heard the gossip. Reginald Clutton-Grey, who had turned fifty, had married for the third time comparatively recently, and to a girl little more than half his age. Kathleen Clutton-Grey had been a well-known television presenter, a profession which, in the eyes of her new mother-in-law, made her quite unsuitable as a wife for Reggie. Moreover, though Kathleen had an attractive, pleasant personality, she was a determined woman, and had no intention of playing second fiddle to the dowager. If Constance Clutton-Grey didn't approve of the alterations she wanted to make to the house and its décor, or of the friends she chose to entertain, that was too bad; Constance could live elsewhere. Kathleen, unlike her predecessors, was not to be the one to be brow-beaten into departing.

'You should know,' Dick Band couldn't resist remarking. 'About women, I mean. Your experience is greater than mine.'

Clutton-Grey chose to take this comment as a joke, and burst into laughter, but before he could think of a suitable riposte, they were interrupted by six-year-old Jeremy offering them a bowl of nuts. The small boy was distracted as they stretched out their hands towards the bowl, which tipped alarmingly. Both the bowl, and its contents would have been on the floor, if Jeremy's father had not come hastening to his rescue. Band liked Susan's husband,

Andrew Hill, who was a large rugger-playing type and a teacher at the nearby public school, Coriston College— pronounced, in a typically English fashion, 'Corston' College—but he noticed that Mary was throwing him appealing glances from the far side of the room, so he made his excuses and went to join her.

Mary, he found, had got herself cornered by Gavin Drayton. Gavin was as unlike his brother Peter as was possible. He was shorter and squarer, resembling his Aunt Helen more than any other member of the family, but he wasn't bad-looking. He had been a studious boy, always interested in puzzles and mathematics. He had done well at school, got a good degree at London University and now, at thirty, had an excellent job with a computer firm in Oxford.

But, if he lacked Peter's vices, he also lacked Peter's easy charm. He was certainly no conversationalist, unless one happened to be knowledgeable about computers, or at least interested in their inner workings and their quirks and what he called 'expert systems'—apparently his latest project. Other topics usually produced only monosyllabic replies. Mary Band, whose acquaintance with computers was limited, was clearly bored stiff with Gavin; she was glad when Dick joined them.

By now several of the people who had come to have a glass of sherry or wine as a gesture had left. Those who remained began to drift, at Helen's request, into the dining-room, where a cold buffet was laid. The Reverend Timothy Merle hovered at one end of the table for a few minutes, obviously wondering if he should say grace. Finally he decided that no one was interested, and proceeded to fill his own plate. The wake—though that scarcely now seemed the word for it—was continuing.

It was four o'clock before the last cousin had gone, leaving only the immediate family to survey the debris. Apart from little Jeremy, who was fast asleep on Helen's bed, there were seven of them. Paul Drayton stood at the open french windows thinking about Muriel Fayne and watching his two sons stroll around the garden together. Ostensibly Peter and Gavin were getting some air. In fact, they were earnestly discussing their grandmother's will.

'The house to Aunt Helen. That's fair, considering how much she did for Gran,' Gavin said. 'The rest divided between Mum and Aunt Helen.'

'We're forgetting the thousand to the church,' Peter remarked. 'I bet the Rev. Tim was expecting more. He'll have been disappointed. So am I. I wish she'd left me that thou.'

'A thousand isn't much use.'

Peter hooted with laughter. 'There speaks the rich man. I'd find it damned useful. Which reminds me, dear brother. You wouldn't care to lend me twenty, would you?'

'No.' For once Gavin was firm. 'You haven't paid me back what you borrowed last month yet—or the month before that.' He glanced towards the house. 'Look out, here's Dad. He won't think it seemly that we're discussing Gran's money on the day of her funeral.'

'Why not?' Peter demanded. 'Dad's probably thinking about the money too—and how little Mum's going to get.'

And indeed Peter was right. Paul Drayton had also been disappointed when he learnt how small the residue of the estate would be. No one had known that some years ago Muriel Fayne had bought herself a fat annuity, so that most of her money would die with her. As far as Paul himself was concerned, the Galleries were prospering and his financial circumstances presented no problems, but he knew that his wife liked money for its own sake, and the children could certainly do with more.

'Tea'll be ready in five minutes,' he called, and returned to the sitting-room.

At once he regretted that he hadn't joined his sons. Biddy and Helen were alone. Sounds from the kitchen suggested that Susan and her husband were making the tea that Biddy, declaring herself exhausted, had requested. And Biddy and Helen were in the middle of an argument.

'I simply don't understand you, Helen.' There were two spots of colour high on Biddy's cheeks, and her voice was sharp. 'What on earth is the point of you keeping the house? It'll be much too big for you. A smaller place nearer Colombury, or even an apartment in the town, would be far more sensible for you, and the children could make use of some of the surplus furniture and things.'

Helen was obviously failing to respond. 'I'm attached to the place, and Mother *did* leave it to me,' she was saying obstinately.

'I'm fully aware of that. But you know how much the Clutton-Greys would offer for it? It seems ridiculous . . .' Biddy turned to Paul for support. 'We're talking about South Winds,' she explained unnecessarily.

Paul nodded. He had foreseen some trouble on this subject, but was not inclined to take sides. 'Surely it's up to Helen to decide,' he said weakly.

The return of Peter and Gavin from the garden, coinciding with the arrival of Andrew and Susan with a tea-tray and a plate of cakes, brought the conversation to an end, to the relief of both Helen and Paul. Helen felt a warning twinge of indigestion and, as only family were present, took from her handbag the plastic tube in which her tablets were presented, popped a couple in her mouth and swallowed them.

Susan said, 'Jeremy calls those things you're always taking "Aunt Helen's sweeties".' She laughed.

'I hope you told him they weren't for him,' Andrew said at once.

'Of course.' Susan was superior. 'I said Mummy would

be very, very angry if he ever touched them, as they were bad for small boys.'

'In fact, I doubt if one would do him any harm,' Helen said, 'though I don't suppose he'd like it much.'

She sat at the table on which Andrew had placed the tray, and began to pour the tea. It was what she would have done even when her mother was alive, but today the act was different and somehow symbolic. It was her house, now that Muriel was gone, and she—Helen—was for the first time the true hostess to a family gathering. She looked around and felt affection for each one of them. Sometimes they annoyed her, as Biddy had just done over the house, but she wouldn't have been without them.

CHAPTER 4

Helen was feeling unwell, and this annoyed her. On this beautiful September day, six weeks after Muriel's death, she found it especially irritating. The formalities were all over —the inquest, as expected, had recorded a verdict of 'accidental death'—and Helen was just beginning to enjoy her lack of responsibility. It was wonderful, for instance, to be able to accept invitations without first referring to Muriel, to decide by herself that she must have the sitting-room redecorated, to have lunch at the Windrush Arms in Colombury instead of dashing home to cope with her mother. But now, at this pleasantly crucial moment in her life, she seemed to have caught this damned bug that was going about.

Helen tried to choke back a sneeze as a couple of potential customers came into the Galleries. Friday afternoons were always busy, and there were already several individuals or couples looking around. The phone had rung about five minutes ago and Paul, who should have been helping her in the showroom, had retreated to the office to take the call. Peter, who was at the far end of the shop, couldn't really be trusted to act suitably, especially if a customer proved a little difficult. Helen blew her nose hard, swallowed to ease her sore throat and went up the spiral stairs to see if she could sell a picture.

'It's a delightful print,' she said.

She was speaking to a well-dressed middle-aged couple who had been standing in front of a Picasso drawing for some time, studying it from different angles. They had already asked the price, and were clearly interested. They returned her smile.

'It's rather slight,' the man said. 'Two wavy lines and the suggestion of an eye.'

'It *is* a Picasso,' Helen pointed out. 'It's a print, of course, but it's numbered and signed. There's no doubt it'll increase in value.'

'Maybe.' The man was shaking his head, unconvinced. 'He did so many like it. After all, it's scarcely more than a doodle. I doubt if it took him two minutes.'

They smiled at Helen again, and turned away. When they had all descended to the main floor, the woman said, 'Thank you,' over her shoulder as Helen opened the street door of the Galleries for them. Helen failed to return the smile. She was angry with herself for having missed the sale. She didn't believe it was the price—which was high, but not unreasonable—that had dissuaded the couple. It had been her own dryness, her lack of enthusiasm. She ignored a girl who was hopefully holding up a ceramic ash-tray, and went across to Paul as he came back into the showroom.

'You've been ages on the phone,' she said accusingly. 'Who was it?'

'Sorry, Helen, but it was Biddy. She . . .' Paul stopped,

looked harassed. 'I'm afraid you're not going to be very pleased about this.'

'About what, Paul? For heaven's sake!'

'It's—it's that trip to the Caribbean Biddy and I were planning for next February. Well, there's a friend of Biddy's who's also going there with her husband, and Biddy wants to go at the same time. It's the second week in January.'

'But that's impossible!' Helen's sallow cheeks flushed with anger. 'Surely you told her—surely she realizes—'

'She knows it's a bad time, but—'

'A bad time!'

Each year, when Christmas was over, the Galleries had a sale, followed by a week during which they shut for stocktaking. This week, which meant long hours and hard work for Helen and Paul, with what help they could get from the family, was invariably the second in January, when the weather was usually poor and trade slack. It had become an accepted annual routine, and indeed from the point of view of business it was important that the period of closure should remain constant from year to year; quite apart from customers, salesmen and manufacturers' representatives knew what to expect.

'Helen, my dear, I'm sorry.'

'Paul, it's impossible. You can't be away then. You can't let Biddy change your trip from February.'

'But she has. She's been to the travel agent and fixed everything. She's determined to go with these friends.'

Helen stared at her brother-in-law in disbelief. She was angry, very angry. For a moment she could have hit Paul. Biddy was selfish. She always had been spoilt and selfish. And Paul . . .

A cold voice interrupted them. 'Are you interested in selling me this vase, or would you rather gossip?'

Helen swung round. She took a deep breath and sneezed, once, twice, three times. The paroxysm gave her precious seconds in which to control her temper. She didn't care that Mrs Wilkinson was giving her a supercilious stare.

Mrs Wilkinson was not one of Helen's favourite acquaintances, but since she had taken up riding, she had met her occasionally at the Derwent Stables, where they both hired horses. Helen did her best to make time to hack around the countryside for a few hours most Saturday mornings. Lorna Castle and her husband, David, who now ran the stables, had been very kind to her, teaching her to ride, if not well, at least comfortably and safely, and always reserving for her a nice, quiet mare—Vain Glory by name—for her Saturday-morning outings. Helen had come to find the rhythmic exercise in the fresh air incredibly relaxing.

Hastily Helen collected her thoughts; at this moment Mrs Wilkinson was a customer.

'You'd like the vase? Of course. It's very elegant, isn't it?' she said. 'Is it for a present? Would you like it gift-wrapped? Paul, you'll look after Mrs Wilkinson, won't you?'

Giving each of them a meaningless smile, Helen retreated to the office at the back of the Galleries. She found some aspirin and took three. Her head ached, her throat was like sandpaper, her nose already sore and, in the mirror, she could see that her eyes were red-rimmed and watery. At this rate, she thought bitterly, there'd be no riding for her tomorrow.

She sat down and rested for a minute, feeling utterly miserable. Biddy had been thoughtless and inconsiderate in changing her holiday to the second week in January, but it was done now, and it was useless to blame Paul. Somehow the stocktaking would have to be achieved without him. It wouldn't be easy, but Peter must be made to do some real work, and perhaps Gavin would help in the evenings, and maybe Andrew . . .

After a few minutes she returned to the Galleries. Paul was on the phone. He grimaced as he replaced the receiver.

'That was Jean Slinter,' he said to Helen. 'According to her, her husband's in London and won't be back till next week, though I swear I saw him coming out of the Windrush Arms at lunch-time today. She insists there's no problem about the money they owe us, and of course we'll be paid. She can't imagine why we're making such a fuss.'

'Because it's a hell of a lot of money, did you tell her?' Helen said.

'It would have been a waste of breath. I did my best to point out that there was such a thing as cash flow, but she said that was nothing to do with her. Frank coped with all the finances.' Paul shook his head. 'She was really quite nasty.'

'If they don't pay by the end of the month, we'll get a lawyer's letter written,' Helen said, 'but it's embarrassing when local people are involved. And it does us no good to seem to be dunning customers, though God knows why we shouldn't.'

'Helen, about Biddy—' Paul began tentatively.

'Forget it, Paul. I'll manage somehow.'

'At the moment you don't look as if you could manage anything, Helen. You ought to be in bed.'

'It's this wretched bug. It's come on awfully suddenly. I'll be all right, but I'll leave early if you and Peter will cope.'

'Of course,' Paul said, and frowned. His ear had caught a sudden change in the tone of Helen's voice, and his gaze followed hers to where Peter was bending over a glass display case. 'What is it?' he asked sharply.

'Nothing.' Helen's response was automatic. Relieved, she heard the doorbell tinkle and saw Kathleen Clutton-Grey come into the Galleries. 'There's the Clutton-Grey,' she said quickly. 'You deal with her, Paul.'

Letting Paul go forward, Helen moved without any appearance of haste to where Peter was standing, his back to

her. 'What are you doing?' she demanded. 'Why have you
opened that cabinet?'

Peter jumped and dropped the key. He grovelled on the
floor to find it. When he got to his feet he was smiling and
composed. He didn't wait for Helen to repeat her question,
but answered at once. He's had time to get his story ready,
Helen thought uncharitably; she had few illusions about her
nephew.

'Lady Clutton-Grey said she'd be looking in this afternoon. She wants to buy a birthday present for a friend, and
I thought one of these bits of silver jewellery would be just
the ticket.'

Helen knew he was lying. She had always known when
Peter was telling fibs, even when as a small boy he had
been given to producing extraordinarily truthful-sounding
excuses. But she didn't want to make an issue of it. Her eyes
flicked over the pieces of silver and, assured that everything
was as it should be, she held out her hand for the key, and
made a show of testing the locked cabinet. 'Each of these
pieces is unique, you know, Peter, which makes them quite
valuable. It wouldn't do for any of them to go missing.'

Without another glance at Peter, Helen went to speak to
Kathleen Clutton-Grey, who had chosen a ceramic bowl
that Paul was wrapping for her. She didn't mention silver
jewellery. Peter had followed her, and Helen knew he would
intervene if he felt it necessary to justify himself.

Kathleen Clutton-Grey greeted Helen warmly. 'Hello,
how are you?' She smiled. 'My husband's planning to come
and see you very soon.'

'Is he? Is he thinking of buying something special,
or—?'

'You could say so.' Lady Clutton-Grey picked up a por-
celain owl from a table, examined it carefully and replaced
it. 'My dear, you know we're hoping to buy your house. As
soon as all the formalities about your mother's will are

complete, and South Winds is legally yours, Reggie will be along to make you an offer, and I assure you it'll be an excellent one.'

An approach of some kind like this was no more than Helen had expected, and she had her answer ready. 'I'm sorry but, however good the offer, I'm afraid it'll be refused. It would be a waste of Sir Reginald's time. The fact is, I've no intention of selling South Winds.'

'But you surely can't be thinking of living there alone? That would be absurd. It's not a large house, but it's much too big for one person. You'd be infinitely better off in a smaller place, nearer to Colombury and your business. And, as I say, Reggie really is prepared to pay well over the odds.'

Maybe it was because she was now feeling decidedly ill, or maybe it was the result of a trying day, or perhaps her ladyship's tone had sounded too patronizing. Whatever the reasons, Helen Fayne forgot that the Clutton-Greys were good customers. She glanced away for a moment, then pursed her lips, and glared at the attractive young woman standing before her.

'I don't give a damn how much your Reggie's prepared to pay!' she burst out. 'South Winds is not—repeat not—for sale, and it won't be as long as I'm alive. So please understand that, both of you.'

For a moment Kathleen Clutton-Grey's face registered nothing but amazement. Then her expression changed. It became hostile and vindictive. 'Don't you be so sure of yourself,' she said to Helen. 'If you're not sensible you might be compelled to change your mind, and you wouldn't like that.' Turning on her heels, she marched out of the Galleries, ignoring the beautifully-wrapped parcel that Paul was holding out to her.

'Whew!' Peter said, and laughed. 'You'd better take care, Aunt Helen, or she'll be inviting you to dinner, saying all is forgiven, and putting poison in your soup.'

'You've got a lurid imagination, Peter.' Helen spoke lightly, but she was shaken. She leant against a table, suddenly shivering, hoping she wasn't going to faint. Then Paul was holding her by the arm, supporting her, and the Galleries steadied. 'I—I'm fine,' she said.

'No, you're not.' Paul was firm. 'It's stupid to pretend you're well, when obviously you're not. You've got this wretched virus or whatever it is. Peter's going to drive you home right now and stay with you till the doctor comes. I shall phone Dick Band at once.'

Helen nodded, and then wished she hadn't as a sharp pain shot through her head. She thought of being tucked up in bed, warm and comfortable and sleepy, and the temptation was irresistible. She did her best to smile.

'All right,' she said.

CHAPTER 5

By Monday most of her friends and acquaintances in the neighbourhood of Colombury knew that Miss Helen Fayne had caught the current virus. She had been forced to cancel her usual Saturday-morning ride, she hadn't put in an appearance at the Galleries in the afternoon and, most unusually, she had failed to attend church on Sunday. There was a great deal of sympathy for Helen. True, her tongue was sometimes somewhat acid, and she tended towards impatience with what she considered to be the stupidity of others, but on the whole she was well-liked and highly respected in the community.

Mrs Ferguson, who had found her duties at South Winds considerably less demanding since old Mrs Fayne's death, actually arrived for work some minutes early on Monday morning. She found Helen, who was feeling much better thanks to the antibiotics Dr Band had prescribed, in the kitchen making tea.

'You shouldn't be up, Miss Fayne,' she said at once. 'If you get up too soon, the next thing you know you'll be really ill again. Now, back you go to bed, and I'll bring your breakfast tray.' She lifted a restraining hand, as if Helen were about to protest. 'No bother at all, it isn't.'

Meekly, Helen went. Thoroughly miserable, she had not enjoyed the weekend. The bug was bad enough, but Dr Band who had been to see her on Friday evening, had paid her a second visit on Sunday and this had not proved altogether reassuring. The doctor had read Helen a lecture on taking more care of herself; he had urged her to relax, to be a little self-indulgent, and not to let others—by whom she knew he meant members of her family—take advantage of her.

'You're not as young as you were, Helen, and you've worked hard all your life,' he had commented. 'Now's the time to ease off. With your mother gone you don't have the same responsibilities. Take a good holiday. Paul can cope with the Galleries. Put yourself first for once.'

Mrs Ferguson, busying herself in the kitchen, would probably have proffered much the same advice. But, unlike Dick Band, who considered it his duty, Mrs Ferguson didn't feel it was her place to do so. In any case, she knew that any such advice would be a waste of breath, so she kept her thoughts to herself. Instead, she made tea and toast, arranged a tray, and as a last-minute thought went into the garden and cut a rose, which she put in a slender glass that was one of Helen's favourites.

Pleased with herself and the gratitude that Miss Fayne had expressed, Mrs Ferguson set to work. She dusted and swept and vacuumed on the ground floor. When she went up to collect Helen's tray, she found her asleep, and nodded her approval. Careful not to wake her, she took the tray and, later, instead of vacuuming the stairs as she had intended, she just brushed and dusted them.

Then the phone rang. 'She's sleeping, Mr Drayton. Sleeping like a baby, she is. Seems a pity to wake her.'

'Yes, of course. It's not important. I'll ring—'

'Paul, I'm here.' Mrs Ferguson had forgotten the extension phone by Helen's bed, which had naturally awakened her. 'Thank you, Mrs Ferguson,' Helen added.

Mrs Ferguson said nothing, but put down the receiver in the hall. She wasn't one for listening to other people's calls. Anyway, through the window she had caught sight of the parson, the Reverend Timothy Merle, in the garden. He was standing by the boarded-over lily-pond, and appeared to be staring at it as if mesmerized. Mrs Ferguson waved and then called to him. As she told her friend the postmistress later, he immediately jumped in the air as if someone had let off a squib beneath him.

Nevertheless, when he came into the house he was quite calm and composed. 'Good morning, Mrs Ferguson,' he said. 'Miss Fayne wasn't in church yesterday, and I'm told she was not well. I'm so sorry. How is she today?'

'A mite better, but still poorly, sir. Would you like to see her—she's in bed—or shall I tell her you happened to call as you were cycling by?'

'Actually I don't have my bicycle. I walked across the fields from the vicarage. It only takes a few minutes that way.'

'Yes, I know.'

Mrs Ferguson spoke as if her words had some particular significance and Timothy Merle glanced sharply at her, but she was merely studying a broken thumbnail. He said, 'I don't want to disturb Miss Fayne. Please just tell her I called to inquire, and if there's anything I can do I'll be only too happy—'

'Yes, I will. I'm sure Miss Fayne—'

She stopped suddenly as there was a sound in the rear hall, and a bluff voice called, 'Hello. Anyone at home?'

Sir Reginald Clutton-Grey came into the kitchen. He was carrying a small silver tureen covered with a cloth, and he placed it carefully on the table. He nodded at the vicar and smiled at Mrs Ferguson.

'Hope you don't mind my walking in, but the door was open, as usual. You never seem to give a thought to burglars at South Winds.'

'We don't have all the valuable paintings and silver and things you've got at the Hall, sir,' Mrs Ferguson said.

'Plenty to steal here, nevertheless. Anyway, I brought Miss Fayne some homemade pheasant soup.' Clutton-Grey gestured towards the bowl. 'Give her my regards, will you, and tell her we hope she'll be better soon. She's not up yet, I take it?'

'No, sir, though I found her getting her breakfast when I arrived this morning.'

Clutton-Grey grunted. 'Well, look after her.' He turned to Merle. 'Come back to the Hall with me, and have a glass of sherry before lunch, Tim. There's something I want to discuss with you.' And, as they were leaving, having said goodbye to Mrs Ferguson, she heard him add, 'It's about Helen Fayne. She oughtn't to be living alone in this house—'

Mrs Ferguson went upstairs to deliver the various messages to Helen. She said she would be leaving after lunch as usual, but she could pop in during the evening if Miss Fayne would like her to. Helen refused.

'Thanks a lot, Mrs Ferguson, but my sister's coming over later, and probably my niece, Mrs Hill, too, so I'll be fine. Besides, I'm feeling a great deal better. I think I might even dress this afternoon.'

'Very well, Miss Fayne, but take care and don't do too much,' Mrs Ferguson repeated her warning.

In fact, Helen didn't get as far as dressing, but she came downstairs, a flannel gown over her nightdress, and she sat by the french windows in the sunny sitting-room, just as her mother had done not many weeks ago. She was surprised how weak she felt. She told herself that, in spite of what Dick Band had said, she really must make an effort. It was important to return to the Galleries as soon as possible.

She frowned unseeingly at the lily-pond, her thoughts elsewhere. On the telephone that morning Paul had told her that it looked as if the takings at the weekend had been ten pounds short. It could be an accounting or arithmetical error, of course, but . . . Helen wished she didn't distrust Peter so much. If only he would settle down and get a proper job, or else take a real interest in the Galleries. He wasn't a boy any more and . . .

'Hello, Aunt Helen.'

Helen started from a brief doze. 'He—hello, dear.' Gavin was the last person she expected to see on a Monday afternoon. He had come in the previous day—after all, he didn't normally work on Sundays—but Biddy had been there, and he hadn't stayed long. Helen had put his visit down as a duty done. But a second call now, on a working day? Her mind still full of Peter, she looked inquiringly at her other nephew.

Gavin pulled up a chair, but angled it so that he didn't look out of the window at the garden and the boarded pond. It was a warm day, but not unduly hot. Yet Helen could see drops of perspiration on his upper lip as he shifted uncomfortably in his chair.

'Aunt Helen,' he began and then, as if steeling himself, said in a rush, 'Aunt Helen, I'm thinking of starting my own business. The market's wide open at the moment for computer software. I know I've got a good job, but I'm sure I've gone as far as I can with the firm. If I'm ever going to strike out on my own, now's the time.'

'That's interesting,' Helen said, not because she was especially interested, but because Gavin seemed to have run out of words. 'It's a risk, I suppose, but obviously if you believe you can make a success of it . . .'

'I can make it successful,' Gavin interrupted with confidence. 'But on one condition. I must have a reasonable amount of capital to start with.'

'Ah!' Helen said.

'Aunt Helen, I'm not asking you to give me any money. I'm not a—a cadger, not like old Peter. It would be an investment for you. You could be my fellow director and . . .'

'Gavin, stop! And please listen to me. I've got no money available to invest and, if I had, I wouldn't put it into computers. Is that clear? I suggest you try your parents, or the banks.'

Gavin Drayton stood up. He regarded his aunt with an anger that he didn't bother to conceal. He said, 'Of course, if it had been Peter, or dear little Susan, they could have had the money, but because it's plain, dull, hard-working Gavin . . .'

'Don't be a bloody fool!' The shocked expression on Gavin's face gave Helen a momentary satisfaction, of which she was at once ashamed. She said gently, 'When I die, Gavin, everything I own will be divided equally between you and Peter and Susan. But until then, apart from the odd small present, I don't propose to finance any of you, or lend you money—and that's final.'

'Well, thanks for making the position so clear.'

Gavin strode—stormed, rather—out of the room, pushing past Susan whom he found standing in the doorway. She came forward slowly and, as Helen greeted her, took her brother's seat.

'I'm sorry, Aunt Helen,' she said. 'I couldn't help hearing what you were saying to Gavin.'

'It doesn't matter. I only hope you don't want to borrow any money to start your own school, or some such venture.'

'No, no. Andrew's very happy at Coriston. Of course, he'd like to have a House of his own, instead of being an assistant housemaster. It would make a lot of difference to us, but there's no hope of that for a while yet.'

She sighed heavily, and Helen, looking at her with quickened interest, noticed her red-rimmed eyes and flushed cheeks. 'Susan, is something wrong? Have you been crying?'

Susan shook her head. 'I'm just being silly. I'm sure we'll cope. Only—Aunt Helen, Andrew will be absolutely furious when he hears.'

'Hears what? What's the matter?'

'I saw Dr Band this afternoon. The results of my proper tests have come through and . . .'

'What tests?'

'I'm pregnant. I'm going to have another baby. I knew it. I tried one of those do-it-yourself tests last week, but I didn't want to say anything till I was absolutely certain.'

Relief that Susan wasn't suffering from some dreadful complaint made Helen less sympathetic than she might have been. She said briskly, 'That's wonderful. A very good thing. It's a pity you didn't have another child years ago, then there wouldn't be such a gap after Jeremy.'

'That's all very fine, Aunt Helen, but babies are expensive items, and we just can't afford another one. Besides, there's not room in our cottage, and we'll never find anything else. Housing within reasonable distance of Coriston is impossible unless you pay the earth. You know that. I can't imagine what we're going to do.'

Helen said nothing. Susan was looking at her watch, clearly impatient to be gone. It was equally clear why she had come; like Gavin, she wanted financial help. Caught up in her own problems, she hadn't even asked if her aunt was feeling better. Now she abruptly said that she must fly, or she would be late picking up Jeremy from school. She kissed Helen briefly, and hurried away.

Helen, who had found both Gavin and Susan exhausting, resigned herself to getting her own tea but, as she was about to make the effort, Biddy arrived. Nor had she come empty-handed. She had brought a homemade cake and some chocolate biscuits. Helen felt disproportionately grateful.

'I was telling Paul that he and Peter will simply have to cope without you in the Galleries until next week,' Biddy said cheerfully. 'It's absurd that the two of them can't manage on their own. Don't you agree, Helen?'

Helen hesitated. 'Peter isn't very knowledgeable,' she said, 'and mistakes can cost money.'

'He'll learn,' said Biddy.

'He could, if he set his mind to it.' Helen refrained from adding that another difficulty was Paul's own lack of business sense which, without her guidance, meant that they bought unacceptable or over-priced stock, and lost on the resale. 'Anyway, I hope to be back at least part-time by Thursday or Friday.'

'You shouldn't rush. This bug leaves one feeling horribly weak. I know it knocked all the stuffing out of me when I had it. I'm not sure you shouldn't take a couple of weeks' holiday. If you don't mind my saying so, dear, you look as if you could do with a rest.'

'Oh, don't fuss, Biddy.'

Helen spoke half-crossly. In fact, she was pleased. Her sister wasn't usually so considerate. She remembered Biddy's determination to make her trip to the Caribbean during the Galleries' annual stocktaking—a subject they had tacitly agreed not to discuss—and told herself to be philosophical about it. After all, Biddy owed her nothing, and it was thanks to Biddy that she had a family. Families were sometimes irritating, but their value was great.

*

Helen Fayne went to bed shortly before nine o'clock. Paul Drayton had looked in earlier, on his way home from the Galleries with Peter, and the three of them had had a drink together. Peter, who was quite a good cook, had made her an omelette for supper. She had watched a television programme, read a little, and decided she'd had enough. She went upstairs.

A hot bath, a strong whisky, and her usual antacid tablets, and Helen was soon asleep. She slept heavily, snoring gently. At one point her snores grew loud, or some extraneous sound disturbed her, because she woke with a start and sat up in bed. She was sweating.

She turned on the bedside light and looked at the clock. To her surprise it wasn't yet eleven. She listened, but the house was quiet. She got out of bed, put on her gown and padded to the bathroom. On her return she drew the curtain, and gazed for a moment out of the bedroom window, but it was a cloudy, starless night and there was little to see except dark shapes. She returned to bed and was asleep again almost immediately.

In the morning it was raining. Helen woke early. The long night had refreshed her, and she was confident she had no temperature. For the first time in days she actually felt hungry; the thought of bacon and eggs tempted her. She washed her face and hands and cleaned her teeth at the washbasin in her room, but she didn't dress, though the house was cold until the central heating took hold. In gown and slippers she set off downstairs.

Most of Helen's clothes were practical rather than elegant. Her nightdress was inexpensive, made of some synthetic material, and too short for her, so that it scarcely reached her ankles. Her flannel gown was also short, and only covered her knees. Her slippers were flat. There was nothing in which to catch a heel, or trip herself.

But on the second step from the top of the stairs Helen Fayne lost her balance. She grabbed vainly at the banister, but couldn't save herself. She pitched headlong down the staircase into the hall below.

CHAPTER 6

It was unusual for Dr Band to be at home at nine o'clock in the morning on a day that he was on duty. It was even more unusual for him to be washing and shaving at such a late hour. But he had been up since two at a difficult maternity case, and had just reached home. Mary was cooking him his breakfast before he belatedly set off on his rounds.

The ring of the telephone, never heard with pleasure in a doctor's household, was even less welcome than usual. Mary answered in her most businesslike voice, prepared to redirect the caller to the Colombury surgery, or to one of Dick's partners. But, as she heard what Mrs Ferguson was saying, she changed her mind immediately.

'All right,' she said decisively. 'Dr Band will be there as soon as he can. Meanwhile, keep her warm, Mrs Ferguson. Cover her, but don't try to move her, whatever you do. You understand? Good. The doctor won't be long, I promise.' Not for nothing had Mary Band once been a nurse.

'Dick!' she called. 'Dick!'

The doctor swore; startled, he had nicked the side of a nostril. 'Yes, what is it, Mary?' he shouted resignedly.

By this time Mary had come to the door of the bathroom. 'That was Mrs Ferguson on the phone. It's not her day for the Faynes, but because Helen's been ill she decided to look in. She found Helen unconscious, in her night clothes in the hall. She'd obviously fallen down the stairs. I said you'd go at once.'

'Of course.'

Dick Band wiped his face. With record speed he finished dressing, seized a piece of toast that Mary had buttered for him, and ran for his car. He drove fast to South Winds.

Mrs Ferguson was waiting anxiously. 'She's not dead, Doctor, praise be. She's come round, and she's able to talk, but I wouldn't let her. I said you were on the way.'

'Good.' Band nodded his approval as he saw the duvet tucked around Helen. He glanced up the stairs. Depending upon the distance she had fallen, she could have hurt herself badly, even killed herself. He knelt down and began his examination. 'Make some tea, would you?' he said to the hovering Mrs Ferguson. 'I expect we could all do with some.'

'Sorry about this, Dick,' Helen murmured. 'It was stupid of me. I was going to get some breakfast and I—I don't quite know what happened.'

'Well, I do.' Mrs Ferguson, having put on the kettle, had returned to the hall. 'I saw when I went upstairs to fetch your duvet, Miss Fayne. You tripped, and it's not surprising. The stair rod, the second from the top, had worked out and the stair carpet's all loose, though how it happened, I can't think. I cleaned the stairs yesterday, and the rods were fine then.'

'I expect I did it as I fell.' Helen was vague. 'I'm sure it wasn't your fault, Mrs Ferguson.'

'Fortunately you don't seem to have done too much damage to yourself,' Band said as he finished his preliminary examination. 'Some bruises. Slight concussion, I suspect, from when you hit your head, and obviously you've hurt your arm. Let's see if you can stand up.'

Carefully Band helped Helen to her feet. She winced as she put weight on her left ankle, but she was able to walk and, with the doctor on one side and Mrs Ferguson on the other, she was soon on the sofa in the sitting-room. She flatly refused to go to the hospital in an ambulance to be X-rayed. She said she would rest—clearly that was essential —and if by the end of the week, when she had completely recovered from her virus, she was still having trouble with her arm or her ankle, she would appeal to the doctor again. But till then . . .

'You're an obstinate woman, Helen,' Dick Band said. 'However, I've not got time to argue with you now. Perhaps if Mrs Ferguson could spare you a few more of her precious hours?' He looked hopefully at Mrs Ferguson, who nodded vigorously. 'Good, then I'll leave you in Mrs Ferguson's hands. But take care, Helen, At present you're not as strong as you might be, and that could have been a nasty accident. You were lucky to get off so lightly.'

'You could have been killed, Miss Fayne. I was reading in the papers only the other day about a woman who—'

Mrs Ferguson continued her monologue, and for once Helen didn't have to restrain the impulse to tell her to be quiet. The flow of words, with their Cotswold burr, formed a pleasant background noise that was strangely reassuring. Helen, still recovering from the shock of her fall, didn't ask herself why she felt a need for reassurance.

It was more than two weeks before Helen was back at the Galleries, and even then she didn't work full-time. She had sprained her ankle and badly bruised her arm, but had fortunately broken no bones. Nevertheless, the fall had shaken her more than she had expected—more than she cared to admit—perhaps because at the time she had been weakened by the after-effects of the viral infection.

During her enforced absence, Paul had kept her well-informed. She knew, for example, that business had been exceptionally good; Peter had worked hard, and on occasion Susan had come in to help. She also knew that the Slinters had not paid the large sum they now owed, and that Paul had foolishly decided to wait another month before taking any action. She knew that the ten pounds which had seemingly been missing from the Galleries' takings had mysteriously reappeared and, though she suspected Peter, she had agreed with Paul to accept the incident as an arithmetical error.

Ten pounds was not in itself a sum of any consequence, especially as it had been repaid. The default of the Slinters and Paul's pusillanimity were of far greater importance. She determined to pay the debtors a visit as soon as the month was over, unless of course they sent a cheque in the meantime. She would have liked to have taken immediate action, but Paul was in a sense the senior partner, and she couldn't countermand what he had already decided.

But there was one item that Paul failed to mention. Helen had instilled in him the basic notion that he must never buy directly from a sales representative, unless the man or woman, or the firm they represented, was known to him. But it seemed that a day or two before Helen was able to leave South Winds a youngish woman with a small child had driven up to the Galleries in an unmarked van. Paul had never seen the woman before, but she had told him a hard luck story, the child clinging to her skirt forlornly, and Paul had bought from her half a dozen rolls of curtain material, which had turned out to be of variable quality. What was more, the rolls when inspected in detail, were far from their stated lengths.

'They probably fell off the back of a lorry,' Peter said, amused by his father's discomfiture in the face of Helen's wrath when she had uncovered these facts. 'Pity I wasn't here at the time. She wouldn't have tried it if I had been. She'd have known I'd have sussed her.'

'You mean it takes a crook to smell a crook,' Helen couldn't resist the comment.

'Now look here—' Peter began.

'For heaven's sake!' Susan exclaimed. 'The point is, what do we do? We've no means of tracing the woman—I bet the address on the receipt is phoney—and if we go to the police there'll be an awful fuss, almost certainly for nothing.'

'I must say I can't see Sergeant Court doing much about it,' Helen agreed. 'But I'd like to see her caught. Stolen or not, it looks to me as if these goods were deliberately made up to deceive, and she could be had for that. You were a fool, Paul!'

Paul Drayton objected—silently—to being dubbed a fool in front of his son and daughter, but he merely shrugged as if to dismiss the accusation. 'She was very convincing,' he said, 'and you should have seen that waif of a child. They certainly needed the money.'

'Maybe, but we don't happen to be a charitable organization,' Helen replied shortly.

'Here's a customer,' Susan intervened, glad to avert what was threatening to become a bitter argument.

'I doubt if he's here to buy anything,' Peter said at once.

Peter was grinning broadly and Susan giggled. Helen gave them a disapproving glance as she went forward to greet the Reverend Timothy Merle. It was immediately apparent that he had not, in fact, come to buy.

'Good morning, Tim. What can we do for you?' Helen asked him cheerfully.

'I—er—it's rather a private matter,' he said. 'I'd hoped to find you alone, Helen.'

'Let's go into the office, then,' Helen said. 'We can talk privately there.'

Helen was fond of Timothy Merle. She was naturally a religious woman; she liked to go to church and, oddly enough, she had much in common with the vicar. She knew he was by no means the eccentric simpleton that many people thought, but a shy, introverted man with surprisingly wide interests, and she enjoyed his company.

'What is it, Tim?' she asked, waving him to a chair in the small office. 'A problem?'

'Not really. It's about the money your—your mother left St Augustine's. A thousand pounds. To be honest, from what she said I'd expected more—and I've spent it.'

'Spent what? How could you? You haven't got the thousand yet.'

'I know, Helen, I know. But it's possible to borrow on expectations, and after all it wasn't for me. It was for the church. I had to have the roof repaired, and the west wall needs repointing . . .' His voice tailed away.

Helen was shaking her head. She felt a twinge of indignation, but ignored it. 'I don't understand, Tim. I'm aware the church has a debt. That's why we have a second collection most Sundays, but you said the bank wouldn't give you a bigger overdraft. Where have you borrowed this money? How could you borrow without consulting the Bishop?'

'It was only from a friend—just for a short time, I thought.'

'A moneylender, do you mean?'

'No. I'm not as stupid as that, Helen. A friend—but now he wants his money back.'

'Why?' He must have known your expectations, as you call them, were vague, to say the least. Mother was strong. She might have lived for years. She might have changed her will innumerable times. People do as they get older.'

'Yes, but—she didn't, did she? And he knows it, and wants his money. You can't blame him. I did promise.'

'How much?'

'Five thousand.' Helen laughed and he stared at her. 'What's funny about five thousand?' he asked.

'It's precisely the amount I've left you—or rather St Augustine's—in my own will, Tim.'

'That's very generous of you.' Merle hesitated. 'But, Helen, it doesn't help right now. Actually I've not spent all the money my friend lent me, thank God, and he'll wait for the thousand from your mother's estate, I'm sure. That means I'm short just two.' The Reverend Timothy Merle took out a handkerchief and dabbed at his upper lip, damp with sweat. 'I hate to ask you, but . . . it would be a loan, of course . . .'

Helen pushed back her chair and stood up. 'I'll have to think about it,' she said. 'On principle, I dislike lending money, even to the church. However—let me see, today's Thursday—I'll give it some thought, Tim, and let you know. By Sunday, at the latest.'

Helen waved aside Merle's thanks. She wished he hadn't asked her, though she appreciated that it was not for himself. Conscious of him close behind her, as if he would have delayed her, she walked swiftly into the showroom. She paused near Paul, who was examining a figurine and moved on, frowning at the sounds of giggling and scuffling coming from the gallery above.

Suddenly there was a piercing scream. Someone shouted 'Look out!' Helen felt a thump between her shoulder-blades and simultaneously she was knocked sideways. Then a large object seemed almost to graze her head as it fell with a crash to shatter on the floor beside her.

For a length of time that seemed far longer than it was, Helen lay on the carpet, aware that both Tim Merle and Paul Drayton were also sprawled beside her. Because she was on her back, she found herself looking up at the two anxious faces peering over the gallery rail. Then Peter and Susan were clattering down the spiral stairs. The vicar, who had been hit a glancing blow on the shoulder, was getting unsteadily to his feet, and Paul helped Helen to stand.

Between the three of them lay the remains of a large, heavy piece of Esquimo sculpture.

There was a chorus of 'Are you all right?' and 'I'm terribly sorry,' and 'Did it hit you?' In the event, it appeared that no one had been badly hurt, though Merle had a nasty bruise and Susan cut her hand picking up a sharp piece of Arctic stone. Helen was suffering only from slight shock.

She pulled herself together. 'What I'd like to know is how that piece—which incidentally is worth quite a bit of money —came to fall over the gallery,' she said grimly. 'The gallery's wide enough, and the railing's higher that the shelf where we display things like this. How on earth could it get up and fly . . .'

'I wanted to move it,' Peter explained quickly. 'It was in the way when we were sorting the prints. I asked Susan to help me lift it—the thing was so damned heavy I couldn't shift it by myself—and she sort of dropped her side of it.'

'No, I didn't.' Susan protested. 'You slipped and jerked it away from me.'

Paul intervened. 'Does it matter exactly what happened? Let's be grateful no one was killed. If that bit of sculpture had landed on Helen's head . . .'

'No thanks to you it didn't, Dad,' Peter said. 'You and Mr Merle practically pushed her under it.'

'Nonsense!' Paul said. 'That's a damned stupid remark, Peter.'

Tim Merle was equally indignant. 'On the contrary! We did our best to thrust Helen out of the way. At least that was my intention, and I'm sure it was your father's too.' He felt his shoulder carefully. 'I would never do anything to hurt Miss Fayne.'

'Of course not,' Peter said, but there was a hint of mockery in his voice.

Helen looked at the flushed faces surrounding her. She

said incisively, 'I suggest we stop squabbling about it, and get the place tidy before someone comes into the Galleries. Peter, you fetch a dustpan and brush. Susan, you go and wash that cut on your hand. I'll leave you to look after things, Paul. I'm tired and I'm going home. Tim, I'll be in touch.'

CHAPTER 7

On Saturday morning it was raining, a thin drizzle that made cobweb patterns on the hedgerows. Helen Fayne was glad that she had decided not to go riding; she had phoned the Derwent Stables the previous day to tell them that she wouldn't be needing Vain Glory. In fact, what with her mother's death and the virus and that horrible fall downstairs, she hadn't been able to ride for several weeks. And the accident at the Galleries seemed to have re-awakened all the aches and pains caused by the fall. What was more, she still doubted the reliability of her ankle.

Throughout these weeks Lorna Castle had of course been most sympathetic, but Helen still felt vaguely guilty. The stables—about ten minutes' drive from her house—were part of Broadfields, the long-time home of the Derwent family, and had once been run by a Derwent daughter. Now the big house was divided into luxury flats and the Castles, who had taken over the stables, lived in one of the smaller ones. Helen knew that David Castle had been invalided out of the army and that, apart from his small pension, he and his wife were dependent on the horses for their livelihood. Too many cancellations couldn't be good for business. Helen resolved that, come what may and regardless of the weather, she would ride the following Saturday; as for today, there was plenty to occupy her.

First, keeping her promise to the Reverend Timothy Merle, Helen wrote him a brief note:

Dear Tim,
  I have given the matter we discussed considerable thought, and it is with regret that I feel I must refuse your request. I cannot lend you the sum you asked for, or indeed any money at all. As I said at the time, I don't approve—She paused and crossed out 'approve', then continued:—believe it's a good idea to lend or borrow money; it may be an old-fashioned view, but I am determined to stick to it.
  I would much prefer to *give* you the money, but unfortunately I cannot afford to do so. Why not try some of the richer members of St Augustine's congregation, such as the Clutton-Greys?

She was tempted to add, 'or the Slinters', but knew that would be unkind. She signed her name, and slipped the letter into an envelope. She would deliver it by hand.

Helen got out her car and drove through the village to the church. She didn't ring the bell at the small house that served as a vicarage, but pushed the letter through the box. Then she continued towards Coriston School, intending to call on Susan.

In three weeks' time Jeremy Hill would be seven. For the past several years he had had a birthday party at South Winds, while it had been his great-grandmother's house. Muriel had welcomed the little guests and had then left Susan and Biddy and Helen to entertain them. The annual party had meant a great deal of extra work for Helen, who organized the event, prepared most of the food and bought —though she didn't pay for—the presents that each child traditionally took home.

So far this year nothing had been said about Jeremy's

party. Muriel's sudden death and its consequences, followed by Helen's illness and accident, seemed to have driven it from everyone's mind. It had been Mrs Ferguson who reminded Helen that the date was approaching.

Helen parked her car in the lane and walked up the narrow path that led to the Hills' cottage. As she rang the bell she inspected the small front garden with its neatly mown square of grass surrounded by a tidy flower border. No one answered the bell, and after a moment Helen went into the house.

There was no hall; the front door opened immediately into the living-room, and it was impossible for Helen to retreat, or pretend she had come upon an ordinary, happy family scene. Susan and Andrew stood facing each other, obviously stiff with anger. They were both flushed, and Susan's cheeks were tear-stained. They turned together as they became aware of Helen's presence. Together they glared at her and, momentarily, Helen sensed that she was in some way the object of their joint tempers.

She hesitated, then said mildly, 'I'm terribly sorry. I did ring the bell. I didn't mean to burst in on you.'

'We—we didn't hear it,' Susan stammered. 'We—we were just—'

'—having an argument,' Andrew interrupted. 'Useless to try to cover up, my dear Susan. It's obvious to the meanest intelligence that we were having a bloody good row, and Aunt Helen's a clever woman. You can tell her why. I'm off to the school. I'm late as it is. I'm meant to be supervising some wretched paperchase.'

Without kissing his wife or saying goodbye, Andrew Hill slammed out of the cottage. Susan began to cry again as she heard the roar of her husband's departing motorbike. Helen sat down, and gestured to Susan to sit beside her.

'Well, tell me what it's about—if you want to,' she said quietly.

'It's—it's the new baby, of course. I was sick this morning, and I had to tell Andrew. He's furious. He said it was my fault, and I suppose it was.' Susan sniffed loudly. 'I ran out of pills, and didn't bother for a week when I thought it was safe. He says three people are bad enough in this cottage without a baby crying all the time.'

'Then he'd better look for somewhere else, or consider building on here,' Helen said shortly. 'Many young couples would be glad to have this place.'

'I suppose you wouldn't like it, Aunt Helen? We could swap.' Susan blew her nose aggressively, as if to refute her aunt's implied criticism of her husband.

Helen ignored the question, and decided to change the subject. 'I came about Jeremy's birthday,' she said. 'Incidentally, where is the boy?'

'In his bedroom, looking at some comics. There's no room here for him to play.' Susan was sulky.

'He ought to be outside in the garden. It's stopped raining.' Helen refused to be sympathetic. 'Anyway, about his birthday—would you like to have his party at South Winds, as usual?'

'Yes, I suppose so. We certainly can't have it here, can we? And Mother won't want it. She'd be afraid the kids would break something or hurt the furniture. South Winds would be marvellous, only . . .'

'Only what?'

'Well, before, Gran always paid for the party, and Andrew and I can't afford it, not this year. We've got to do our best to save for the new baby.'

Helen hid her amusement at the obvious nature of Susan's ploy. 'Don't worry about that,' she said. 'I'll pay, my dear.'

'Will you, Aunt Helen? That *is* kind of you,' Susan said, as if the idea had never occurred to her.

For the next half-hour they discussed Jeremy's birthday party—the food, the favours, the gifts for the guests. Then a friend of Susan's, the wife of another master, dropped in, and Helen left. She drove to Colombury, deciding that if the Galleries were not too busy she would go on into Oxford, treat herself to lunch at the Randolph Hotel and try to buy some of the items needed for the party.

At the Galleries, she was surprised to find Biddy helping Paul. Biddy rarely came into the shop, except to chat or buy a small gift. Today she was serving two teenagers who wanted a present for their mother. Paul was attending to an elderly lady. There was no sign of Peter.

When they were free, Helen explained her plans for a trip to Oxford. She half expected an objection from Biddy, but there was none. In fact, Biddy agreed that she would gladly work in the Galleries for the rest of the day.

'If you're prepared to have that ghastly party for Jeremy, it's more than a fair return,' Biddy said. 'One small boy dashing around the house is bad enough. A whole troop of them—plus small girls, who are often worse as far as I can see—is unthinkable. It would be a nightmare.'

Helen laughed. 'Where's Peter?' she asked.

'Entertaining a girlfriend from London,' Paul said. 'That's why Biddy's standing in for him. Incidentally, Helen, I saw our lawyer yesterday and he's going to send the Slinters a stiff letter next week, demanding payment and threatening legal action.'

'Good! We've given them plenty of time. If anything, we've been over-generous. And we need the money to pay our own bills.'

A customer appeared and Paul went to attend to him. Biddy walked to the door with Helen. The drizzle had stopped, and it was now a bright day.

Helen said, 'If it had been like this earlier I might have gone for my Saturday ride. Whatever the weather I must go next week, or poor Lorna Castle will be worrying about her cash flow too. She loses money if I don't turn up, because she always keeps Vain Glory for me. If I don't take the mare she's out of pocket.'

'You should have taken up golf,' Biddy said. 'Much more sensible than hacking round the lanes by yourself. You'd have met a lot of people at the club. Potential customers.'

'I leave that side of the business to Paul,' Helen said lightly, wondering if her sister's remark had been a reminder that Paul's contribution to the success of the Drayton Galleries was not negligible. 'He's very good at it,' she added generously.

'I know,' Biddy replied crisply.

But his socializing didn't make up for his frequent idiocies, Helen thought as she got into her car. Paul's folly in buying those rolls of over-priced and under-length material from an unknown woman because he felt sorry for her child still rankled. Helen had been horrified to learn how much he had paid for the goods, and she hadn't yet decided what to do with them. She had no intention of selling such sub-standard material in the Galleries.

Brooding on the problem, Helen drove into Oxford. She parked the car, and went straight to the Randolph. She had a whisky in the bar, then entered the dining-room. The hotel was buzzing with activity and she was lucky to get a table, even if it was tucked away into a cramped corner. She gave her order and, foreseeing that there might be some delay, asked for another whisky.

She enjoyed her drink, and the meal, with which she had a carafe of house wine. Regretfully, bearing her weight in mind, she refused cheese—not after profiteroles with cream, she thought—and settled for black coffee. She didn't hurry. It might be selfish, but she was giving herself a treat, and had all the afternoon in which to do her shopping. She drank her coffee, poured herself a second cup and looked around the dining-room.

Suddenly she was still. At the far end of the room she

noticed for the first time a table occupied by three people, a man, a girl and a child. Helen moved her chair slightly to see them better. The man was unquestionably Peter Drayton; Helen recalled that he was meant to be entertaining a girlfriend from London. The girl, auburn-haired, and smart in a jade-green suit, was a stranger to her. But it was the child Helen found most interesting.

The little girl—for it was a girl—had her back to Helen, but her face was reflected in a large wall mirror. It was an appealing face—thin, with white skin powdered with freckles, enormous eyes and a wide, drooping mouth. Framed in jaggedly cut red hair, it was the face of a waif. Helen caught her breath as the comparison came naturally to her. At present the child was wearing an attractive dress, but in other clothes . . .

Helen finished her coffee and paid her bill, adding a generous tip. She now regretted her luncheon. She wished she had never made the trip to Oxford, never seen Peter with the girl in the green suit and the waif-like child. But what was done couldn't be undone. Possibly it was the two whiskies and the wine which strengthened her resolve, but she decided that matters—like her suspicions—couldn't be left to stew.

Nevertheless, it was with some reluctance that she made her way between the tables to where the three of them were sitting. 'Hello, Peter!' she exclaimed, with forced brightness.

'Aunt—Aunt Helen!' Peter pushed back his chair and got to his feet. For a moment he looked panic-stricken, his Adam's apple rising and falling as he swallowed. Then he regained control and managed to smile. 'What a pleasant surprise! Carol, this is my Aunt Helen—Miss Helen Fayne—who owns the Drayton Galleries in Colombury with my father. Aunt Helen, Carol Bryant and Patsy.'

It seemed to Helen that Peter's introduction had been unnecessarily explicit as far as she herself was concerned, but very meagre as regards the Bryants, and she realized immediately that his words could be interpreted as a warning. She shook hands with the girl and the child, and found that at close quarters both of them were older than she had originally guessed.

'How do you do, Mrs Bryant,' she said.

'*Miss* Bryant.'

'I'm sorry. Miss Bryant, Peter didn't mention it, but I believe you have an interest in the textile business too—curtain material, that kind of thing.'

'Then you believe wrongly, Miss Fayne.'

'Mummy's an actress. Like me. We're resting just now, but . . .'

'Aunt Helen—please!'

They all spoke together—the girl, the child and Peter—and Helen glanced from one to the other. She was not unkind, and she didn't blame the Bryants. She knew only too well how persuasive Peter could be, too persuasive for his own good, she thought sadly.

She said, 'If you'll excuse me, Miss Bryant, Patsy, perhaps Peter would see me to my car.'

They smiled their goodbyes. As Helen turned away Peter cast his eyes heavenwards in a theatrical gesture, but he meekly followed his aunt. She stopped when they reached the pavement outside the hotel, and waited for him to speak.

At least Peter didn't try denials. He said, 'Aunt Helen, it was a joke—on Dad. I knew I wouldn't have got away with it if you'd been in the Galleries.'

'It was *not* a joke, Peter. Granted, you made your father look a fool, but that was irrelevant. It was a deliberate—and successful—attempt at fraud, an attempt that apparently you planned. It was dishonest, possible deserving a prison sentence if charges were pressed. I don't know. But I do know that I never want to see you in the Drayton Galleries again. That's all I've got to say. Goodbye.'

Helen turned and walked away. She went to her car and sat in it for several minutes before she started the engine and drove home. She no longer felt capable of shopping; she was too miserable.

On Monday morning Helen arrived early at the Galleries, but Paul, whom she hadn't seen since their brief meeting on Saturday, was already there. In order to avoid the family she had purposely chosen the eight o'clock communion service the previous day.

As soon as she saw Paul's face she knew there was going to be trouble. He looked tense and anxious and she braced herself for an argument. He followed her into the office, where she went to take off her coat.

'Helen!'

'Yes, Paul.' She didn't wait for him to start his explanations, but continued at once. 'I assume that Peter hasn't come in this morning?'

'No. Peter's gone up to London for a few days. A holiday. Biddy gave him the money.'

'Heavens! Do you really think he needs a holiday? Or money, after the amount he stole from us, from the Galleries?' Helen was indignant.

'He didn't steal anything. I was stupid to buy that stuff. Anyway, Biddy and I have decided that we should sell it for what we can get, and I'll make up the difference out of my own pocket. So the business won't be losing anything.' Paul smiled placatingly at Helen.

'You and Biddy have decided, have you? Well, that's nice, Paul, but I don't agree. I'm not having shoddy, second-rate goods sold in these Galleries, and that's flat. Nor is Peter coming back to work here, not as long as I'm around. You'd better see the situation clearly, and accept it for what it is.'

'Helen, please. You *must* forgive him. He's terribly upset about it all.'

'You mean he's upset that he was caught out? Paul, Peter's got to be taught a lesson. Otherwise he's going to commit some serious crime and end up with a long prison sentence. Is that what you and Biddy want?'

'No, of course not. But—' He caught Helen by the shoulders. 'Helen, dear, please! For my sake!'

'No! I'm sorry, Paul, but no!' Helen released herself. 'There's the shop bell. You'd better answer it. I'll phone the *Oxford Mail* and put in an advertisement for an assistant. I think we need one, an efficient one—and honest, too.'

CHAPTER 8

It was not a pleasant week for Helen. In the first place, Paul made no secret of his feelings, and when a second appeal on Peter's behalf had failed he refused to take any part in the process of finding another assistant. Secondly, Helen had no luck with her search. There were several answers to the advertisement in the *Oxford Mail*, but no really suitable candidate emerged; the one girl to whom Helen had rather hesitantly offered the job turned it down.

She saw nothing of Biddy or Susan or any of the family, except Paul, and though this was not extraordinary, it was unusual enough for her to wonder if she were being ostracized. But it was Paul's aloof and distant attitude that perturbed her most, and to her surprise she found that she was missing Peter; for all his faults, her nephew was dear to her. She was thankful when Saturday came round again.

It was a fine, clear morning with a hint of frost—ideal for riding. Helen had an early breakfast, dressed herself in jodhpurs, roll-neck sweater, jacket and hard hat, and set off for the Derwent Stables. Before she left, she took time to write the Castles a cheque to cover her missing hours. Lorna received it most gratefully.

'It's terribly kind of you, Miss Fayne, but it's not in any way necessary, you know. Mrs Wilkinson took Vain Glory out on two of the Saturdays, so the mare wasn't completely idle.'

'That's splendid,' Helen said. 'How's David?'

'Not too bad. He's teaching Jean Slinter to trot at the moment.' Lorna laughed at the thought. 'Mrs Slinter's a bit scared of horses, but she won't admit it, though her mounts know, of course. I'd have put her up on Vain Glory if you'd not been coming. It might have given her more confidence. Vain Glory's such a gentle beast.'

'I didn't know that Mrs Slinter rode,' Helen said.

'She's only just started.'

Helen made a sound that suggested muted interest. She was thinking that the Slinters might have paid some of their debts to the Galleries before Jean took riding lessons, which were far from cheap. Then Mrs Wilkinson drove up.

Lorna Castle said, 'I'll be taking out a small party in a few minutes, Miss Fayne. Would you like to wait and come with us, as it's some weeks since you've had a ride?'

If Mrs Wilkinson hadn't obviously been going to be one of the party, Helen might have agreed. But she remembered the Wilkinson woman's rudeness the last time she had been in the Galleries and said, 'No thanks, Lorna. I'd rather go by myself. I'll be fine on Vain Glory. I'll just go my usual round, nice and quietly.'

'It would be difficult to do anything else on that mare,' Mrs Wilkinson said, overhearing them as she joined the couple. 'I can't imagine who gave her that inappropriate name. She's like an old armchair.'

The description was not entirely accurate. True, Vain Glory was an elderly mare with a placid disposition, but she remained a most attractive creature. She was a chestnut with a black mane and tail, and Helen was attached to her. When Lorna led her out Helen rubbed the mare's head and produced two lumps of sugar from her pocket. Then, ignoring Mrs Wilkinson, she mounted, somewhat heavily and stiffly, and with a wave of her riding-crop—an implement she carried more for show than anything else— rode out of the yard.

When Helen said that she would go her usual round, she meant it literally. There were variations when she was feeling adventurous but these were trivial. Today, as was her custom, she set off through the grounds of Broadfields until she came to a lane beside the church of St Mary the Virgin. A little further on, she turned on to a bridle path and continued via tracks and lanes until she reached the western boundary of the Clutton-Greys' estate.

She met one man walking his dog, and two children picking blackberries. Otherwise she was left to her own thoughts. Inevitably, they were not particularly happy. She was worried about Peter—both about Peter himself and the family's reactions to what had happened. She wondered once again if she might have been too harsh, if she should have listened to Paul . . .

Resolutely she thrust these thoughts from her. Instead, she made herself consider her garden, the need to prune the roses, to plant a flowering shrub where one had died, to plan for next Spring. Vain Glory ambled peacefully along.

Finally, slightly more contented, Helen kicked the horse into a trot, and then a gentle canter. But neither rider nor horse was eager for violent exercise, and soon they agreed to subside once more into a quiet walk.

Eventually they turned into a lane, wide enough for farm tractors and equipment and bordered with high hedges. Beyond the hedge on one side was the Clutton-Greys' estate, while behind the other were fields. Between the lane and the fields was a wide grassy verge that might have been designed for walkers or riders.

Helen sat squarely in her saddle, her hands loose on the reins. Often she liked to trot along this stretch before she turned for the stables and home. This morning, mindful of how stiff she would probably be the next day, she let the mare continue to walk. She was thinking now about Jeremy's birthday party, and was quite unprepared for what happened.

Without warning Vain Glory bucked, lashing out with her back legs. Then she gave a plaintive whinny and suddenly set off at a gallop. Somehow Helen managed to hang on. She had naturally been thrown forward, and had lost both stirrups. Blood was streaming from her nose where she had hit it on Vain Glory's poll. She had dropped her riding-crop, and with one hand clung on to the horse's mane, while with the other she tried unsuccessfully to recover the reins.

They came to the end of the lane. Instinctively and without hesitation Vain Glory swerved to the right in the direction of her stables. By now they were on a tarmac road, with Cotswold stone walls on either side. The mare's gallop became a canter, then eased to a trot. Reginald Clutton-Grey, who had driven out of his driveway to be confronted by the extraordinary sight of Helen Fayne lying along the mare's back, was able to leap from his car and stop Vain Glory without difficulty.

The mare stood, sweating and trembling. Helen lifted a blood-stained face and, gasping for breath, gave Clutton-Grey what was meant to be a smile. Then she pushed herself upright and, with his help, managed to dismount.

'My dear lady, what on earth happened to you? Did the ruddy mare bolt?'

'Yes. Something must have startled her. I wasn't paying attention, and anyway I'm not much of a horsewoman.'

'There's little one can do if a horse decides to bolt, I can tell you. But you're all right except for a bloody nose, aren't you?' Clutton-Grey was suddenly anxious. 'Can you walk? I don't suppose you want to mount the beast again at the moment. You'd better come up to the Hall, so that we can clean you up. Give you a drink perhaps. And when you've recovered I'll drive you home. The Castles can collect the horse. It's one of theirs, isn't it?'

'Yes,' Helen said. 'It's very kind of you. I'm sorry to be so much trouble.'

'Not a bit. Come along. I'll fetch the car when I've got you to the house. Kathleen'll look after you.'

Leaning on Clutton-Grey's arm, Helen walked slowly up the drive. Her nose had stopped bleeding, but her face hurt and she felt badly shaken, though she had scarcely had time to be frightened. She glanced across Clutton-Grey to Vain Glory walking sedately beside him. She couldn't bring herself to blame the mare. Something had made her act in a way that was completely out of character. But what? There was no obvious reason for her behaviour that Helen could recall. No small animal in her path, no one around. Perhaps, Helen thought, she had been stung by an insect, or . . .

They had reached the house. Kathleen Clutton-Grey wasn't there; according to Reggie's mother she had gone for a walk some time ago, as Reggie should have known. Nevertheless, Helen couldn't have received better care and, almost an hour later, having been given two large brandies, she was driven home. She telephoned Lorna Castle to assure her that neither she nor Vain Glory had come to any harm, and also reassured Paul. Then she went to bed. But Clutton-Grey's last words echoed in her head.

'By jove,' he had said. 'You should take more care, Miss Fayne. You're becoming accident prone.'

*

The next morning, though still stiff, Helen Fayne went to Matins. The congregation was small but, of those present, almost everyone seemed to have heard of her adventure with Vain Glory. She found the many inquiries embarrassing, and blamed the Clutton-Greys for spreading news of the incident. Paul and Biddy assured her that they had told no one, and she didn't think that Lorna Castle, who had been extremely upset and had spent ten minutes on the phone apologizing for Vain Glory's behaviour, would have publicized the event.

'It was nothing much. The mare bolted a short distance, but she soon got tired and stopped. There was no real danger,' Helen said for the nineteenth time.

'You've got a nasty bruise across the top of your nose. That must have hurt,' Timothy Merle said sympathetically.

'Yes, it did,' Helen admitted. She hadn't seen the vicar for over a week, and was glad when he made no reference to her note about money. 'But I can't pretend it spoils my beauty.'

Merle laughed. 'All the same, you should take more care. You've been having too many accidents recently, Helen.'

This repetition of Clutton-Grey's comment disturbed Helen. She nodded a quick goodbye, and hurried after the Draytons. Biddy had insisted she should come home with them for Sunday lunch.

They were waiting for her in the car park and Biddy said, 'Shall I come in your car, Helen? Would you like me to drive?'

'Yes, do come with me, if Paul doesn't mind. But I'll drive.'

The two women got into Helen's car, and Biddy wasted no time. As Helen had suspected, Biddy's request to accompany her was not without an ulterior motive. At once she began to talk about Peter.

'He's in Oxford at the moment, staying with Gavin. He

says it's no fun being in London if you've no money in your pocket.'

'No, I imagine it isn't.' Helen was unforthcoming. Then an idea occurred to her. 'You haven't invited him—them —to lunch today, have you, Biddy?' she asked.

'No, though I considered it,' Biddy admitted. 'Helen, this nonsense has got to stop, you know. Of course Peter behaved stupidly. He realizes that as well as anyone. But it *is* the Drayton Galleries, and Peter is Paul's son. We've told Peter he can come back tomorrow,' she ended in a rush.

'I see. In that case there's nothing more for us to discuss, is there?'

It was only a short drive to the Drayton's house, and neither of them spoke again. Helen was annoyed at the way in which the matter had been taken out of her hands, though not altogether regretful about the outcome. It was true, she thought, that the present situation couldn't continue indefinitely. A lot would depend on how Peter behaved when he returned, she decided.

During lunch they avoided the subject, and talked instead about Jeremy's birthday, the latest television series, local gossip. It was a typical Sunday meal, roast lamb with potatoes and vegetables, apple pie and cheese; Biddy was a competent if unimaginative cook. They lingered over coffee.

Sometimes on these occasions Helen stayed for tea but today, because she felt stiff and in need of some gentle exercise, she left soon after three. She said she intended to go for a short walk when she got home, but once in the car she changed her mind. She remembered the riding-crop she had dropped when Vain Glory bolted.

It was an expensive crop that Paul had given her when she first took up riding. Well cared for, and never used in earnest, it was still like new. Helen was attached to it, and sorry to have lost it. The possibility that it was still lying in the grass waiting to be found was too great to be ignored.

Helen drove to the end of the lane. She parked the car and, glad she was wearing flat shoes, began to walk slowly along the grassy verge. When she came to the point where Vain Glory had bolted she stopped and retraced her steps a few yards. She wasn't sure exactly where she had lost the crop, or exactly how she had lost it. All she cold hope was that she hadn't flung it from her, perhaps over the hedge.

Wishing she had brought a stick she scuffed the grass—thick in patches—with her shoe. There was no sign of the crop. But she persevered until she reached the tarmac road near the entrance to the Clutton-Greys' drive. Then, resigned to failure, she set off back, accepting that someone had seen the crop and picked it up.

Nevertheless, she continued to walk slowly and kept her eyes on the ground. This time she was lucky. Suddenly, quite near the place where Vain Glory had been startled she saw the riding-crop. It was sticking out of the bottom of the hedge, and could easily have been mistaken for a branch. Delighted, Helen bent down and pulled it free. Then she stiffened.

Lying in the grass, a few inches from the crop, was a dart. It was bright and shining, its feathers undamaged. Clearly it had not been outside for long. And it was a strange object to find by the bottom of a hedge.

Tentatively, as if the dart might have a life of its own, Helen picked it up. She wrapped it in her handkerchief and put it in her pocket. Then, carrying the riding-crop, she returned to the car and drove home thoughtfully.

The next morning, before leaving for the Galleries, she phoned the Derwent Stables, with the ostensible purpose of asking after Vain Glory. Lorna Castle said that it was kind of Helen to worry. The mare was fine. She had taken her out on Sunday and intentionally passed along the lane where the incident had happened. Vain Glory had shown signs of nervousness, but hadn't misbehaved.

'I think she must have been stung by a bee or a wasp or something, Miss Fayne. It would account for her reaction, and David found a tiny blood spot on her rump when she was groomed.'

'Did he now?' said Helen. 'Poor Vain Glory.' She wondered for a moment whether or not to mention the dart, but decided against it. The suggestion could only cause a mass of unnecessary speculation.

CHAPTER 9

The week that followed, the week before Jeremy Hill's seventh birthday, was uneventful. Business at the Drayton Galleries remained brisk and Helen was glad to have Peter's help. The newspaper advertisement for an assistant had been cancelled, and Peter was working hard, if somewhat dourly. Paul's obvious pleasure at his son's return also pleased Helen.

And the Saturday of the party was a glorious autumnal day, fine and warm for the time of year. Helen had been up late the evening before, icing the cake, making a huge trifle and ensuring that everything was ready for the great occasion. She enjoyed her work, and woke the next morning with a feeling of pleasurable anticipation.

But she refused to let the prospect of the party and the need for any last minute preparations, or more importantly the remembrance of what had happened on her last outing, deter her from her Saturday-morning ride. At the Derwent Stables Vain Glory, ready saddled, was waiting for her. A couple of other horses were also awaiting their riders, and a third was already mounted.

Lorna Castle was a little over-anxious. 'How are you, Miss Fayne? Do you really want to take Vain Glory again so soon? Have you forgiven her? Are you sure you wouldn't like a change?'

'No, thank you. Of course I'll take Vain Glory.' Helen spoke firmly She had told no one of the dart she had found near her riding-crop, but left it in its handkerchief at the back of a desk drawer. Nevertheless, she had not forgotten it. On the contrary, she had given its possible significance considerable thought, though without reaching any conclusions. 'But if you're going out now, I think I'll join you this time,' she added casually to Lorna.

'Fine!' said Lorna enthusiastically. 'That's a very good idea. We won't be doing anything exciting—I'll have Mrs Slinter on a leading rein—but at least we'll go a different way so as not to remind Vain Glory.'

Helen nodded her agreement. She had hoped to ride beside Lorna, but she didn't relish Jean Slinter's company. Nor was she spared Mrs Wilkinson. Nevertheless, it was an enjoyable outing. What Reginald Clutton-Grey would have called, 'A nice little hack for learners and those who never will learn.'

Remembering this catch-phrase that she had spontaneously attributed to Clutton-Grey, Helen was amused to find his car parked in front of South Winds on her return. Sir Reginald was walking around the garden and clearly inspecting the house.

'Hello there!' he greeted Helen heartily. 'Haven't given up the gee-gees, I see. Good show!'

Helen smiled. 'What can I do for you?' she asked. 'It's early for a drink. Would you like some coffee, Sir Reginald?'

'I should love some. Very kind of you.'

'I'm afraid it'll have to be in the kitchen.' Helen apologized, explaining about the forthcoming birthday party.

While Helen put coffee and water in the percolator, Clutton-Grey gazed around the kitchen with interest. 'It needs modernizing,' he said. 'And I was noticing that your roof's got a bad patch near the chimney. It'll be an expensive repair—scaffolding and all that.'

'I dare say. Everything costs money these days.' Helen was carefully non-committal. She had found two cups, sugar, cream, and had put some chocolate biscuits on a plate.

'Have you come to talk about buying South Winds from me?' she asked without further preamble. 'Because, if so, I must warn you it's a wasted visit. I thought I'd already made it clear that I do *not* intend to sell, Sir Reginald.'

'But this house is much too big for one person, especially when you're out most of the day. It was different when your mother was alive. Now—'

While he drank two cups of coffee and ate three chocolate biscuits, Sir Reginald Clutton-Grey tried every persuasive argument he could dredge up. Admittedly, his attempts at persuasion were amicable, and even Helen, who knew how much he wanted South Winds for his mother, was surprised at the price he offered her; it was at least twice the market value of the place, and for a moment her determination not to sell was shaken. But she loved the house, and the garden she had created. Besides, if she parted with them, where would she live? And she had no real need for extra money.

At last Clutton-Grey shrugged his shoulders. 'All right, if you're adamant, you're adamant, I suppose.' He stood up, and grinned at Helen ruefully. 'Thanks for the coffee, and your company. Before I go may I use your bathroom? You won't refuse me that, will you?'

'Of course not,' Helen said, smiling in return. 'I do understand your situation, and I'm sorry about the house, but there you are. The most I can offer is a first refusal if I ever do decide to sell.'

'Thanks, but by then it'll probably be too late.'

Sir Reginald had spoken gloomily, and Helen didn't need to ask him what he meant. She turned to the sink to wash up the cups, leaving him to go along to the cloakroom. She hoped that this conversation would be the end of the matter. Then, to her annoyance, she heard Clutton-Grey climbing the stairs.

This was by no means his first visit to South Winds. He knew the position of the downstairs cloakroom perfectly well, and had no reason to use the upstairs bathroom— except to pry. Helen thought of going into the hall and calling to him but, with a sigh, decided to take no action until she heard the sound of the flush and steps on the stairs.

But Clutton-Grey had moved so quickly that she had no chance to confront him; he was almost at the front door when she came out of the kitchen. 'Again, many thanks for the coffee—and the use of your—er—amenities.' Suddenly he stopped, with a theatrical gesture. 'How stupid can one be? I nearly forgot, and Kathleen would never have forgiven me. We're giving a party at the Hall on Saturday week, mostly for the neighbours. Drinks, six-thirty to eight. May we hope to have the pleasure of your company?'

'Saturday week? Yes, I'm sure you can, Sir Reginald.' Helen spoke after only a momentary hesitation.

'Good! Look forward to seeing you.'

With a wave of his hand Clutton-Grey departed, leaving Helen to wonder about the real reason for his call. But by the afternoon she had forgotten him.

At two-thirty Jeremy Hill arrived at South Winds with Susan and Biddy, his mother and grandmother, in tow. He was an attractive child, tall for his age, fair-haired and blue-eyed—an inheritance from the Faynes. Normally he was a quiet boy, but today he bubbled with excitement. Helen stopped and kissed him.

'Happy birthday, Jeremy.'

'Thank you. And thank you for my lovely present,' the boy said solemnly.

Helen laughed. She had given him a lifesize yellow ceramic cat, that had seemed to take his fancy in the Galleries; she hoped he really liked it. 'What else did you get?' she asked.

'Mum and Dad gave me a cricket bat and some books. Gran gave me a game and more books. Uncle Gavin gave me one of those calculators that help you do arithmetic. And Uncle Peter gave me Rupert.'

'Rupert?' Helen wasn't sure if Jeremy's broad smile was because he had reached the end of what was, for him, a long speech—almost an oration—or because 'Rupert' (whatever or whoever he was) was the gift that had pleased him most.

'A stuffed bear,' Susan said with scorn. 'Peter has no idea what boys of seven like.'

'I *do* like Rupert!' Jeremy contradicted her. 'He's my bestest present.'

'At his age it should have been a puppy,' Biddy said.

'We never had a puppy when we were young,' Susan reminded her mother sharply. 'And it's the last thing I'd want at present. The new baby's going to be enough trouble. I was sick again this morning.'

Fortunately Mrs Ferguson, who was to help in the kitchen, arrived at this moment, and her appearance put an end to the family bickering. Everyone admired the beautifully-wrapped gifts on the dining-room table, the crackers that had been preserved from Christmas and the cake with its seven candles.

Altogether there were twelve small children at the party, all about Jeremy's age. Some were boisterous and some were shy. Each arrived with a small parcel for their host, and in their tiny but mercenary hearts each was happily anticipating the gift that he or she would receive in return. Soon the party was in full swing, Susan organizing games with Biddy's help. Apart from one little girl, who complained bitterly at the absence of a conjuror, they were all clearly enjoying themselves.

At the right moment Helen called them in to tea. The immense trouble she had taken over the preparation of the meal was rewarded by the 'oohs' and 'aahs' of the visitors when they saw all the pretty and exciting food they were to eat. The cake of course was the *pièce de résistance*, and Jeremy put the crown on the traditional progress of events by succeeding, amid much clapping, in extinguishing all seven candles with one puff.

But soon afterwards in the kitchen Mrs Ferguson said to Helen, 'Young Jeremy's looking tired. He's lost all his sparkle. Too much excitement.'

It was the first intimation that the boy might be unwell. He seemed to have abandoned any pretence at interest in his party and, as parents came to collect their offspring, he paid scant attention to the bustle of departures and the chorus of 'goodbyes' and 'thank yous' and 'happy birthdays'. He appeared half asleep.

'Wake up, Jeremy,' Susan said. 'We'll be going home in a minute.'

Helen intervened. 'Not just yet, please. You must have a drink before you go. Mrs Ferguson will clear up the debris. What would you like?'

Biddy asked for a gin and tonic, Susan for sherry, and while Helen poured the drinks they discussed the party. No one took any notice when Jeremy quietly left the room. He was a good child, unlikely to get into any mischief, and was as much at home in South Winds as in his own house.

The three women finished their drinks. Susan insisted that it was time they went, and they were all on their feet when Mrs Ferguson burst into the room, furiously wiping her hands on her apron.

'It's Jeremy!' she cried. 'He's curled up at the foot of the stairs. I thought he'd gone to sleep, but I can't wake him.'

'Oh God!' Susan said, and dashed out into the hall, closely followed by Biddy and Helen and Mrs Ferguson.

In those first moments of panic, they clustered round the boy, talking to him, even shouting at him, shaking him. Then, when he failed to respond, they grew calm. And, oddly enough, it was Biddy who took charge.

'It must be something he's eaten. Helen, get hold of Dick Band. Mrs Ferguson, make black coffee, and Susan, help me lift him. We must take him to the lavatory and force him to be sick.'

No one argued, though Helen hesitated, aware that this was quite the wrong treatment for certain forms of poisoning. As she dialled the Bands' number she was scarcely aware of the reproachful glance that Susan cast at her, as if to blame her for the incident.

'Yes,' Mary Band answered on the second ring. 'Dick's been out all the afternoon, but he's just come in. Here he is.'

Dr Band listened to Helen's hurried explanation. 'I'll be with you as soon as I can,' he promised. 'Meanwhile, if it's food poisoning you seem to be doing the right thing. He can't have got hold of anything else, can he?'

'I don't think so,' Helen said.

'Oh well, I expect it's the food,' Band said. 'And, Helen,' he added as she was about to put down the instrument. 'If any of you have a moment, check on the other kids who were at the party.'

'Yes, I'll do that myself,' Helen said.

She could hear Jeremy vomiting into the lavatory pan, and assumed that this was a good sign. She reported on her conversation and then, armed with the guest list, went up to her bedroom to telephone. It was a tedious task. There were nine families to contact, and some had not yet reached home. Those who had were anxious and tried to delay matters while they cross-questioned her. She became increasingly abrupt, and finally slammed down the instrument to cut off one mother who wouldn't stop talking.

By the time she had completed her task, Dr Band had arrived and, to everyone's relief, Jeremy was obviously improving. His face was a pasty white and, in spite of being wrapped in a blanket and sitting in front of an electric fire, he shivered spasmodically. But he was awake and fully conscious of what was happening.

'He—he's going to be all right,' Susan said, biting her lower lip to prevent herself crying.

'Thank God for that,' said Helen.

Band, who was preparing to give Jeremy an injection, looked up and smiled at Helen. 'And thanks to everyone acting so promptly. What about the other children? Have you got in touch with the families?'

'Yes, finally,' Helen replied. 'No one else seems to have suffered any ill-effects at all.'

'I'm glad of that, at least,' Susan said.

'Not that it means anything,' Biddy said. 'I once went to a dinner party at which smoked salmon was served. We all ate it, but I was the only guest who was ill later. The doctor said it was quite usual.'

'He was right,' Dick Band admitted, busying himself with Jeremy. 'A minute bit of contaminated food can do the trick, even though the rest of the dish is perfect. Anyway, no great damage done this time. The young man'll be fine in a day or two. Get this prescription filled, and I'll look in on Monday,' he added to Susan. 'Keep him home from school.'

Dick Band left amid a chorus of thanks. Helen saw him to the door. He stopped as he was getting into his car, and said, 'Come and have supper with us next week, Helen. Mary will phone, but it'll probably be Thursday, if that suits you. It's my night off.'

'That'll be lovely. Thank you very much,' Helen said. Two invitations in one day, she thought, remembering the

Clutton-Greys' party—and what a day! She knew she was exhausted.

CHAPTER 10

'Your usual?' Dick Band asked, smiling.

'Please,' said Helen Fayne. 'No ice.'

'He poured her a whisky, added a fair amount of soda and passed her the drink. Professionally he noticed the way her answering smile appeared and disappeared nervously, as if she were not in total control of it, or was too preoccupied to bother with superficial appearances. But he made no comment.

Mary Band said, 'It's just us this evening, Helen. I hope you don't mind. We did ask another couple, but unfortunately she's not well, so they can't come. We didn't want to change the date because we're going on leave next week—up to Scotland. We're looking forward to it so much.'

'Of course I don't mind, Mary. In fact . . .' Helen stopped. She looked from Dr Band to his wife, and gave the same quick, tense smile that Dick had noted. There was a pause as if she were forcing herself to a decision. Then she drank half her whisky in one gulp before firmly replacing the glass on the table beside her. 'In fact, I'm very glad,' she said. 'There's something I want to tell you, to ask your advice about.'

Momentarily she seemed unable to continue, and Mary said, 'My dear, if there's some trouble, we'll do anything we can to help. You know that.'

'I'm not sure you *can* help, but—oh, I've just got to tell someone.' Helen pulled the unattractive magenta-coloured dress she was wearing tight over her knees as she leant forward. 'If I were ten years younger you'd say I was having

my menopause and suffering from delusions, but I'm way
past that. And I'm not imagining anything.' She paused.
Then she added almost casually, 'Someone's trying to kill
me.'

There was a startled silence, as Mary and Dick did their
best to absorb Helen's statement. In the comfort of their
sitting-room, the curtains drawn, the lights bright, familiar
objects around them, it wasn't easy to accept. Band found
himself reflecting for a moment on past cases and unexpected
diagnoses. Nothing was impossible, he knew only too
well.

He said quietly, 'Helen, we have every respect for your
intelligence. We shan't think you're suffering from delusions.
But tell us why you think that.'

'Thank you.' Suddenly Helen relaxed. 'I was afraid you'd
laugh at me.'

'You must have known we wouldn't do that,' the doctor
said. 'If you believe what you say, Helen—and you clearly
do—that's quite sufficient for us to take it seriously. But
you'll have to tell us the whole story.'

'Of course.' Helen finished her drink, and held up her
glass. 'May I?'

Band got up to pour her another whisky, and Helen
began. 'Recently I've had a series of accidents—if they
were accidents. In retrospect I'm far from sure they were,
though . . .'

Naturally the Bands knew of Helen's fall downstairs, and
about Vain Glory's bolt. They hadn't heard of the heavy
piece of Esquimo sculpture that had almost fallen on her
head. And now she told them everything—Clutton-Grey's
odd visit, the dart she had found in the hedge, the spot of
blood on Vain Glory's rump.

'That was what first made me suspicious. Vain Glory
wasn't stung by an insect. It was the dart, I'm positive.'

'But it could have been . . .' Mary avoided the word

'accident'. 'A prank. Boys playing. When the mare bolted they were too frightened to own up.'

'I'd thought of that,' Helen said shortly. She could see the increasing doubt reflected in their faces. 'I wanted to believe it was something like that. But I can't, not any more —not since the business of Jeremy.'

'Jeremy?'

'What do you mean, Helen? What's the connection?'

'Jeremy ate something that made him go to sleep. If Biddy and Susan hadn't acted quickly and forced him to be violently ill, he might not have woken up.'

'Helen, you don't know that. I was there. The symptoms were perfectly consistent with food poisoning.'

'No, Dick, I can't be sure. But I do know that there was one thing Jeremy ate that no one else did. He ate two of what he calls my "sweeties".—the antacid tablets that you prescribed for my indigestion. He might even have had three—I'm not quite sure how many were left in the tube, but it's empty now. He'd found them on my bedside table where I always keep some. Of course he knew he shouldn't have touched them, and he isn't normally a naughty child, but he was over-excited because of the party, perhaps. Anyway, he was tempted and he ate or swallowed some.'

'But even if he did . . .' Band began.

'How do you know this, Helen?' Mary asked simultaneously.

'I know because he confessed to me. He said he knew it was wrong to take them, and he was sure he'd be punished if he told his mother, so he'd kept quiet. Then his conscience began to prick him, so he decided to come to me. I told him he'd been very naughty and he must never do it again, but this time to forget it—it would be our secret.' Helen paused. 'I said my tablets wouldn't have made him ill like that, anyway.'

'Ah,' said Band. 'That's just what I was thinking. Indeed they wouldn't.'

Helen nodded. 'I realized that, Dick. But I suspect a couple of other tablets—probably strong sleeping pills—were substituted for my antacids. I think I was meant to take them with my usual night-cap before lying down.'

Helen left the argument unfinished. Dick and Mary stared at her and each other. Neither knew what to say. She had spoken with such absolute coherence and was so obviously sincere that they made no attempt to pick holes in her story immediately. Nevertheless, the holes were apparent, especially to Dick with his experience as a police surgeon.

'Sleeping pills are usually in capsule form these days,' he offered tentatively. 'But there are some put up as tablets, and I suppose you're so used to taking your own tablets you might not have noticed some slightly different markings. It's a pity they were the last ones in the tube, so that we've nothing to analyse.'

Mary took a different approach. 'Helen, why should anyone want you dead? You must have asked yourself that.'

'Of course I have. I'd hate to think it of anyone.' Helen gritted her teeth. 'As far as I know, I've got no enemies. People may dislike me, but that's in a different category from setting out to kill me. And I'm not a rich woman. When I do die, apart from South Winds and my equity in the Galleries, there'll be a few thousand—a very few thousand—each for my immediate family and for St Augustine's, but that's all. Of course, there *is* South Winds—but no! The idea's ridiculous! I refuse to contemplate it.'

Dick Band glanced at her, as if about to seek some explanation, but Helen continued.

'I *have* wondered if he—or she, or whoever it is—is merely trying to frighten me, though I can't imagine why anyone should want to do that either.'

Helen picked up her glass to find it empty. 'The whole

idea's mad,' she concluded, 'but there's one thing I know for sure—I'm scared.'

'That was not a very happy evening,' Mary commented as she and her husband were tidying up in the kitchen after Helen had left. 'What do you think, Dick? Has she gone round the bend, or—'

Dick Band shook his head. 'I must say I find it difficult to believe there's anything in what she says. She's always been a sensible, intelligent woman, but—On the other hand, if someone really is trying to kill her they're being damned inefficient about it. The fall downstairs. The sculpture bomb. The bolting mare. The substitute tablets. They sound like the titles of Sherlock Holmes short stories. But if anyone was bright enough to organize them all, I'd have expected him to be able to make a nice, clean job of a murder. Why not shoot her in the back, or brain her with a coal hammer.'

'Or drown her in the lily-pond?'

'Mary!'

'Dick, you were the one who first had doubts about Muriel Fayne's death. Remember?'

'Yes, I do now. But I don't see any connection between Muriel's death and these supposed attacks on Helen. Do you?'

'No, not really. But, if there is a murderer at large, it must be someone close to the Faynes, someone who knows their habits and can come and go at South Winds without causing comment.'

'A member of the family, in fact, Mary?'

'Not necessarily. A friend would do. Or an acquaintance like Reginald Clutton-Grey.'

'For heaven's sake, Mary! You're getting as imaginative as Helen. Just because the wretched man went upstairs to pee instead of using the nearest john you make him a suspect.

Anyway, he wasn't in the Galleries when the bit of stone almost fell on her.'

'No, only Paul, Susan and Peter, and Timothy Merle were there, I think,' Helen said.

Dick Band sighed. 'Mary, don't let's start playing detective. If you want my professional—my honest—opinion it's that Helen's taken to drinking a little too much lately, and she's created a drama out of a series of unrelated incidents.'

'All the same, for her sake I wish we could have been more convincingly reassuring.'

'So do I. But apart from keeping in close touch till we go to Scotland there's nothing we can do at the moment—unless she becomes ill, of course.'

Or unless she gets herself killed, Mary Band thought. But she kept her thought to herself.

Although Helen Fayne's invitation to the Clutton-Greys' party had been delivered most casually, she had subsequently received a card. 'RSVP' had been crossed out, and *'pour mémoire'* substituted, which amused Helen as unnecessarily pompous. The Clutton-Greys gave a great many parties in the course of the year, usually for their London friends with a very small complement of neighbours. Every so often, however, they restricted their invitations to local people and their families. This was such an occasion, and thus a relatively unimportant affair.

Nevertheless, unimportant or not, Sir Reginald had organized a formal receiving line—himself, his wife and his mother—at the entrance to the long drawing-room at the Hall, which was easily able to absorb the fifty or so guests. If Sir Reginald were over-hearty, too nearly the Lord of the Manor entertaining his tenants, few people minded. Either they were gratified, or they thought him a joke. Only the occasional guest objected.

'Bloody man,' Gavin Drayton said. 'Who the hell does he think he is? He's just been talking to me as if I were a clever schoolboy dependent on him for my scholarship money or something.'

'Nonsense,' Helen replied. 'He's just keeping his end up. He doesn't have a clue about computers, but he's not prepared to admit it. Anyway, Gavin, if that's how you feel, why did you come? You know what our host is like, and there was no compulsion.'

'He came for the booze and the scoff.' Peter laughed. 'The food's always jolly good here, and with a bar at one end of the room you can have as much as you like without anyone noticing. So let me get you a drink, Aunt.'

Gavin scowled at his brother who, with a wave of his hand, went off to the bar. Gavin said, 'I'm home for the weekend and the parents brought me. But it was you I wanted to see, Aunt Helen. I wondered if you'd had any second thoughts about my new business.'

'Planning to go it alone, are you, young man?' It was Frank Slinter who, with his wife, Jean, had come up to them unexpectedly. 'Very dicey at this time, very dicey, I'd say. I wouldn't recommend it.'

'I'm sure you wouldn't, Mr Slinter,' Helen said icily. 'Nor would I, unless I were certain I'd be able to meet all my commitments.'

Hoping they would take the hint, Helen deliberately turned her back on the group and walked away. She spoke to Lorna and David Castle for a few minutes and, when Mrs Wilkinson joined them, passed on to other groups. She had a brief chat with her sister, then sought out Timothy Merle who, she thought, had been avoiding her since her refusal to lend him money.

'—so many cars streaming up the drive when I arrived,' he was saying. 'I felt positively unsafe on my bicycle. I can't think why no one is capable of walking fifty yards these days.' He turned to greet Helen. 'I'm sure *you* didn't come by car, Helen.'

'I most certainly did,' Helen said. 'I know our properties adjoin, and there's a short cut from the grounds of the Hall to South Winds. Sir Reginald takes it sometimes, but I never do. It means clambering over a wall. Otherwise, it's quite a long way round to the front entrance, much too far for high heels at any rate.'

'Yes, of course. High heels. I never thought of that,' Merle said. He chose a sardine on toast from the tray of canapés being offered to them and ate it quickly, so that he had time to take another before the tray was removed. He smiled apologetically. 'I had no lunch,' he explained.

Helen looked at her watch. 'I'll be going shortly, Tim. If you'd like to follow me, I'll give you supper.'

'Supper?' His face brightened. 'That would be delightful. Thank you.' He held out his hand. 'The least I can do in return is get you a drink.'

Automatically Helen gave him her glass. 'Just one more weak whisky and soda,' she said.

Earlier she had seen Susan and Andrew arrive, among the last guests to do so; probably their baby-sitter had been late. So far she had had no chance even to wave at them, but now, as the groups of people formed and reformed, there was a sudden gap among them and Helen had a clear view of Susan and her husband.

Susan was wearing a blue taffeta dress with a low scooped neckline, and with her fair hair gleaming looked very pretty. As Merle left her. Helen made her way across the room to the Hills, who were talking to Kathleen Clutton-Grey.

They chatted for a few moments, and then Paul and Biddy appeared, with Merle behind them. In one hand the vicar held the whisky he had fetched for her and in the other a plate of canapés.

What happened next was not entirely clear. Perhaps,

turning at Paul's voice, Helen jogged the vicar's arm. Whatever the cause, the result was a shower of canapés, partly
over Susan and Andrew, but mostly over Helen herself.

Typically, there was immediate confusion. Susan was
upset and Andrew was angry. Helen seemed to make light
of the incident, hastily brushing herself down, but she was
clearly not pleased. Reginald Clutton-Grey, hurrying to the
scene, issued orders to the servants. Other guests clustered
around. And Timothy Merle got in everyone's way. But the
whole episode was over in two or three minutes.

Helen, a little irritated by the fuss, found in her hand the
whisky that Timothy Merle had brought her. She drank it
down quickly, and said she really must go. But there were
various delays. Goodbyes and thanks had to be said; the
dowager Lady Clutton-Grey kept her talking. She staggered
once, as she was leaving the room.

Paul, who was with her, said, 'Helen, are you all right?
Should you be driving? Would you like Peter . . .'

She glared at him. 'I'm fine.'

Reginald Clutton-Grey saw her to the door, and watched
her wend a somewhat uncertain way towards her car.
Timothy Merle was at his elbow, waiting to say goodbye.
Clutton-Grey waited, watching, till Helen had shot off down
the long, winding drive, with Merle, supper on his mind,
pursuing her on his bicycle. It was a funny sight, but he
wished Helen had remembered to fasten her seat-belt. Still,
she was only going a few yards, he thought and, shrugging,
he returned to those of his guests who remained.

The party was in fact breaking up. People were already in
the hall, and the front door was open when Merle returned,
pedalling furiously up the drive. He leapt off the machine
and let it fall to the ground with a crash. His face was ashen,
his suit covered in blood and he gasped for breath.

'Accident!' he spluttered. 'Accident! Helen failed to take
the corner out of the drive. She drove straight into the stone

wall opposite. She's—she's impaled on the steering-wheel.
I tried to free her but I couldn't.' He turned away, and
before anything could be done vomited over Frank Slinter's
highly-polished shoes.

.

CHAPTER 11

'It's a dreadful shock,' Mary Band said. 'I can't believe it.
There we were in Scotland, playing golf and enjoying our
holiday, and Helen was dead. We didn't even go to the
funeral. No one told us.'

'No reason why they should,' Band said. 'We weren't
relations, and when I rang the surgery to ask if all was well
I only spoke to the locum, who had no idea Helen was a
friend of ours.'

The Bands had returned home late that day. Mary had
thought of telephoning South Winds, but had decided to
wait till the morning. Dick, however, had phoned his partner, and had learnt the details of Helen Fayne's death. They
were both distressed by the news.

'I'll make some tea,' Mary said, and sighed as she went
into the kitchen, followed by her husband. 'It's such a short
while since she was having supper with us and told us—'
Mary stopped, the full kettle in one hand.

Dick took it from her and plugged it in. 'Mary, there was
nothing wrong with the car, if that's what you're thinking.
The car—or what remained of it—was examined afterwards, as a matter of course. It has to have been an accident.
Helen was by herself, and she'd been drinking quite a lot at
the Clutton-Greys' party. There were plenty of witnesses to
that. And they did· do a PM, you know, which showed
alcohol in her stomach and blood, though not enough to be
over the limit, I gather.'

.

'I dare say. Helen did drink, probably more than was good for her, but I've never seen her even mildly tipsy, let alone drunk. Have you, Dick?'

'No, I must admit I haven't. But it only needs one careless move when you're driving, and—'

'I know,' said Mary sadly. The kettle boiled and she made the tea. They sat opposite each other at the kitchen table. In spite of the hour, neither of them felt like going to bed immediately.

'I wish we'd been there—at that party, I mean,' Mary said suddenly.

'Why? What could we have done?'

'I don't know. Perhaps prevented another accident, as you call it. After all, Helen did warn us what might happen, but we didn't believe her, did we? And now she's dead.' She paused, then added inconsequentially, 'I wonder if she ever got the two postcards we sent her from Scotland.'

Dick reached across the table and took Mary's hand. 'My dear, it's no use reproaching ourselves. There was nothing we could have done, and there's nothing we can do now. I tell you, the incident has been written off as a traffic accident. You don't expect me to go round asking questions, do you?'

Mary shook her head. 'No. Please don't. It might be dangerous.'

Dick Band looked up sharply and laughed, though his laughter sounded a little forced. 'You genuinely believe that someone tried and tried, and eventually succeeded in causing Helen's death?'

'Yes, I do,' Mary said simply. 'Helen was an intelligent woman, and she'd worked out that someone wanted her dead. We should have listened to her with more—more understanding.'

'Maybe. But there wasn't much to go on, was there? Anyway, as I said before, there's damn all we can do about it now.'

'There *is* one thing, Dick. We could ask George and Miranda to supper. We owe them a meal in any case, and at least it would calm my conscience if we told George the whole story. If *he* agreed that there was nothing to worry about, that Helen must have just been accident prone, I'd be able to forget it, I think.'

There was an appreciable pause before Dick Band answered. He was torn between a wish to do as Mary suggested—such an approach would help to resolve his own small but nagging doubts—and a reluctance to involve George Thorne. But finally he said, 'Okay, tomorrow you try to arrange a date with them.'

It was never simple to arrange a date with the Thornes. Detective-Superintendent George Thorne of the Thames Valley Police Serious Crime Squad, based at the Kidlington Headquarters just north of Oxford, was an extremely busy officer. His working hours were long and erratic, and any private engagement he undertook was liable to be cancelled at the last moment. His friends had learnt to accept this, and most of them sympathized, not least the Bands who naturally faced somewhat the same problems themselves.

However, a date was fixed, and there was no call from Miranda to say she was 'terribly sorry, but . . .' In fact, it so happened that Thorne had just completed a case, and was as free as he ever was. He and his wife arrived on time, and ready to enjoy the evening.

The Thornes were, perhaps, an unusual couple. In their forties, and childless—a fact neither of them regretted—they were devoted to each other. But the attraction must have been that of opposites. George was a man of medium height, with a trim, straight-backed body, fair hair, grey eyes and a neat military moustache. He was often taken for an army officer, rather than an extremely competent detective-superintendent.

Miranda's appearance was also deceptive. She was a plump, attractive woman with a round face, dark curly hair and brown eyes. She looked a happy housewife, as indeed she was, but superficially no one would have taken her for an intellectual. In fact, she had hidden depths. She composed crossword puzzles and acrostics which she sold regularly to the quality papers and weekly reviews. Tonight she was wearing a bright red dress, which Mary duly admired.

Miranda smiled at the compliment. She loved bright colours. 'It matches George's socks,' she said in a supposedly confidential whisper. 'He doesn't really like them, but it's good for him to wear something cheerful occasionally.'

This remark, which the two men had heard quite clearly, set the tone of the evening. The Bands had agreed beforehand that they wouldn't broach the subject of Helen Fayne until dinner was over. Instead the conversation was confined to holidays, the new car the Bands needed, mutual friends, the Government's latest stupidity and other general topics. But after an excellent meal with a good bottle of wine Band asked Thorne if he would mind talking shop for a while.

'Something worrying you, Dick?' asked Thorne, who knew his friend only too well.

'And me,' Mary intervened before her husband could reply.

'Okay,' Thorne agreed. 'Tell me all. I'll help in any way I can.'

Mary poured coffee, while Dick gave George Thorne a snifter of cognac before he began to speak. The tale took some time, as he had not only to explain Helen Fayne's series of accidents, but also to outline the characters and relationships of all the individuals who had been involved in one way or another. Mary delayed matters, too, by intervening now and then to emphasize a point.

'I'm almost certain that I once met Helen Fayne and Paul Drayton,' Thorne said unexpectedly as Band came to the end of his story. 'I was passing through Colombury and I bought Miranda a small gift at the Galleries. But that was a year ago. The people didn't really register.'

He fell silent, and Band had to ask, 'Well, what about it, George? What do you think? Are Mary and I being fanciful? Was Helen Fayne being fanciful, for that matter? Should we forget the whole thing?'

'I don't know,' Thorne said candidly. 'These presumed accidents do seem a bit much to be merely a series of coincidences, don't they? On the other hand, if they were serious attempts to kill they were pretty inefficient.'

'That's exactly what I said,' Band pointed out, glancing at Mary.

'An amateur job,' suggested Miranda, 'but finally successful?'

There was a pause before Mary said thoughtfully, 'You know, listening to Dick recount what Helen told us, I find I'm more than ever convinced that she was murdered.'

George Thorne didn't contradict Mary. Instead, he said, 'As so often, it could well come down to a question of *cui bono?*—who's gaining by her death? And as far as I can see, almost everyone is, though perhaps trivially. The niece and the nephews share the residue of the estate, and the parson can pay off his debts. Even these Slinters might get extra time to pay off theirs—though that's surely very weak. The house—what's it called, South Winds—could easily be sold to Clutton-Grey, so he gets what he wants. What happens to Helen Fayne's partnership in the Galleries?'

'I've no idea,' said Dick. 'I haven't seen the will. All I know is what Helen told us, and she wasn't explicit about that point.'

'Well, anyway, if we're looking for motives, let's suppose Paul Drayton and his wife have a chance to buy Helen's share, and thus get complete control—'

'That's a dicey thought,' interrupted Mary. 'You must

remember that it was Helen who made the Galleries as successful as they are. Paul knew this perfectly well; he depended on her judgement. She'll be hard, if not impossible, to replace. Incidentally, Paul's dreadfully upset at her death, poor man. I've not seen Biddy, though of course I wrote as soon as we learnt what had happened and I got a very friendly letter back. But I did go into the Galleries when I was shopping in Colombury and I thought Paul looked dreadful, as if he hadn't slept for a week.'

Mary poured more coffee, and George Thorne held up his glass for another brandy. 'Miranda'll drive,' he commented, to give himself time to think.

The Superintendent had a great respect for Dick Band's judgement, and it was apparent that both the doctor and his wife were worried. But the Thames Valley Police had enough work to do without looking for more, and this could turn into a messy, time-consuming case—if there were a case at all.

Finally he said, 'There's certainly no shortage of suspects. It's evidence that's lacking, and likely to remain so. You're never going to prove someone deliberately loosened that stair rod, nor that it was Helen who was meant to be brained by that chunk of sculpture—if anyone was. The same probably goes for the bolting mare; we don't even have the dart Miss Fayne said she found. Of course, we know the place and time of that incident, so alibis might eliminate some suspects. I'd say the best bet would be to try to trace the tablets that were supposedly substituted for Miss Fayne's antacids, and the drug you've implied was put in her drink at the Clutton-Greys' party. But there's absolutely no proof that either the substitute tablets or the other drug ever existed. What's more, as far as the accident's concerned, there still remains the question of drink as the cause. Maybe Miss Fayne didn't have a great deal to drink; it could still have been enough.'

Thorne found the silence that followed this dissertation slightly embarrassing. He was aware that he had disappointed the Bands, but he had given them his honest opinion. He couldn't see it as a police job, not unless something further turned up.

He told them this, and concluded, 'I'm sorry. I realize she was a friend of yours, but—'

Dick Band nodded his acceptance of Thorne's opnion. 'It's okay, George. I understand. It was good of you to let us pick your brains. But, as you say, Helen was a friend, and she came to us with this—this story. I wasn't imagining things all by myself, as I did with old Muriel.'

'Who was old Muriel?' Miranda asked, glad of a chance to steer the conversation away from Helen Fayne.

'Muriel? Muriel was Helen's mother. Biddy's mother,' Mary Band said in surprise. 'Didn't we make that clear?'

'You explained about Helen, why she had come to live with her mother, and that her mother had died fairly recently, but you didn't mention her name,' Miranda said carefully.

'And you didn't say that you'd had—shall we call them doubts—about her death, Dick,' put in Thorne.

With some reluctance Band recounted how Muriel Fayne had drowned in the lily-pond, and why he had at the time found her death somewhat puzzling. 'I'm not sure why,' he admitted. 'It was just a funny internal feeling that she should have been able to get herself out of a few inches of water, arthritis notwithstanding.'

'Interesting,' George Thorne said, wondering if the 'something further' had indeed been handed to him. 'If the mother hadn't been dead, the house wouldn't have been Helen's to sell, assuming she would have been prepared to. What's more, I guess the house has increased the value of her estate by a good deal.'

'It would seem to let the Slinters out,' Miranda remarked. 'They'd have nothing to gain.'

But Thorne had ceased to listen. He was thinking. His instincts had at last been aroused. Here, surely, were too many inexplicable factors. He couldn't believe that both Helen Fayne and her mother had been accident prone. The whole affair was beginning to smell.

Finally he said, 'I'll tell you what I'll do. The first chance I get, I'll put the matter to my Chief Constable. If he agrees, we'll look into both deaths. Maybe nothing will come of it, but you never can tell.'

The next morning George Thorne kissed his wife goodbye rather absently, and set off for work. It was a fifteen-minute drive from his neat suburban house to Kidlington. As usual, he turned into his parking space exactly on time, and as usual found a pile of paperwork awaiting him on his desk.

What with the daily briefing he was forced to attend, the over-night files he had to study, a short report he had to prepare, and constant interruptions from other officers and the phone, it was late morning before he had time to contact the Chief Constable's secretary, and ask when it would be convenient for him to have a word with the Chief.

To his surprise, she said, 'Come along right away, Superintendent. He's free at the moment. Someone who was coming in has cancelled.'

In fact, when Thorne reached the Chief Constable's office, Philip Midvale was on the point of completing a telephone conversation with someone in the Met at Scotland Yard. He waved Thorne to a chair, and hung up. 'Well, what can I do for you, Superintendent?' he asked.

Thorne came to the point at once. 'You know of Dr Band, sir. He's one of our most respected police surgeons. He's also a friend of mine, and he tells me that he believes it possible—he stresses the word possible—that he has unearthed a case of double murder in the village of Wind-field, near Colombury.'

'Ah!' said the Chief Constable.

The sound was intended to convey interest, but no commitment. Philip Midvale was a heavily-built, slow moving man, but there was nothing wrong with his intelligence and acumen. He appreciated that Detective-Superintendent Thorne was one of his best officers, whose successes far outstripped his failures, but he didn't find him a totally compatible colleague.

He would never have suggested it, but privately he considered Thorne one of the more 'difficult' officers with whom he had to deal. In Midvale's opinion, the Superintendent, while giving full value to the conventional, plodding part of police work, was too apt to rely on some peculiar sixth sense. And too often Thorne seemed to feel that this—call it 'intuition'—justified him in bending the rules. That Thorne was usually right didn't make this quirk any easier for the Chief Constable to accept.

But Philip Midvale did his best to be fair. 'Before you brief me about it, Superintendent, tell me this. Do I take it you agree with Dr Band? You also believe it's a possibility —a good possibility?'

George Thorne knew that his answer was important— perhaps a turning point in the discussion—but he didn't hesitate. He had lain awake a large part of the night reviewing the situation, and had made his decision. 'Yes, sir, I do,' he said.

'I see,' said the Chief Constable somewhat resignedly. 'So what's the story?'

Thorne wasted no time, but retailed the details of the case as succinctly as possible. Midvale listened in silence.

It was one of the Chief Constable's virtues that he made up his mind quickly. 'Very well, Superintendent,' he said. 'I'll agree to a preliminary investigation. A few questions in the right places may stir things up enough to show if there is a villain. And if there is one, he may make a mistake. It shouldn't prove too difficult an inquiry. You seem to have a plethora of suspects and motives, at least, though in the end you'll probably find there's nothing in it, except perhaps a little too much to drink on this Miss Fayne's part.'

'Yes, sir. Thank you, sir.'

Thorne rose from his chair quickly. He had got what he wanted, and he recognized from the Chief Constable's voice that the interview was at an end. But he wished Midvale hadn't commented on the likelihood that the case might prove simple. In his own experience any case connected with Colombury was likely to turn out as complex as they came.

CHAPTER 12

When Detective-Superintendent Thorne left his house the next morning he warned his wife that it was likely to be a long day, and he would probably not be home until late.

He was to be proved right.

'The Colombury police station first, to pay our respects to Sergeant Court, then the Drayton Galleries, sir?' asked Detective-Sergeant Abbot, as he and Thorne set off from Headquarters in an unmarked car. The Superintendent had briefed his Sergeant on the outlines of the case the previous afternoon.

'Yes. Your old stamping ground,' Thorne agreed.

'I'd scarcely call either of them that, sir,' Abbot said with his soft Oxfordshire burr. 'Colombury—yes. It's what you could call my home town. But not the Galleries. I was never much of a one for arty things.'

'But you knew the late Miss Fayne?'

'By sight, sir. She was what I'd describe as a fierce-looking lady, and opinion in the town was often divided about her. Some said she was an old bitch, but others didn't agree. Some maintained she often did kind and generous deeds without making any great fuss about them.'

'M—mm. Interesting,' Thorne said, and lapsed into thought.

He liked Sergeant Abbot. He knew him as a good and hard-working policeman, and a reliable companion. If possible the Superintendent always chose him to work with, especially if a case involved the people of Colombury and the villages around. Colombury was the town where the Sergeant had been born and brought up, and his local knowledge could be valuable.

The liking was mutual, though the two men could hardly have been more different in character and attitude. Bill Abbot, in his early thirties, was a cheerful extrovert, with a procession of girlfriends, and an unsurpassed knowledge of the pubs in the Thames valley area. He was far from stupid, but he often found Thorne's convoluted thinking difficult to follow, though by now he had become accustomed to his superior's idiosyncrasies.

One of George Thorne's idiosyncrasies—and one of which Bill Abbot thoroughly approved—was a liking for his meals at regular hours, which often wasn't easy for them to achieve when they were on a case. So, as they approached the outskirts of Colombury Abbot risked interrupting the Superintendent's thoughts.

'Sir, perhaps I should remind you that it's market day here, and the place'll be crowded. We'd be well advised to make sure of a table for lunch at the Windrush Arms.'

'Right,' Thorne said promptly. 'I agree. Let's get our priorities straight. Drop me off at the station. I'll make your excuses to Sergeant Court. Then you can park the car and fix things at the pub. I'll meet you at the Galleries.'

'Very good, sir,' said Abbot, hiding his pleasure at the arrangement, which would give him a chance to call on his latest girlfriend, who was a cashier in the local branch of a High Street bank. 'It may take me a while to find a parking space,' he added with guile.

In the event the Superintendent and his Sergeant arrived at the Drayton Galleries at the same time. Thorne had been longer than he expected at the police station. Warned of his coming, Sergeant Court had the kettle ready and a plate of fancy biscuits waiting. Court was an efficient but unambitious officer. However, he liked to please and he liked to talk.

'Everything's fine, sir,' said Abbot, breathless from hurrying after a long chat at the bank. 'The car's parked, and the table's booked. They were full, but I took the liberty of mentioning Dr Band's name, and it worked like magic. What about you, sir?'

'I got some background information,' Thorne said noncommittally, 'and that always comes in useful.'

He opened the door of the Galleries, and they went in. A young man came forward at once. Thorne didn't need Abbot's mutter of 'Peter' to identify him. But he was intrigued by the fact that Peter Drayton's welcoming smile faded rapidly as soon as he saw Sergeant Abbot.

Nevertheless, Peter recovered himself quickly. 'You, I know,' he said, scorning to pretend that he had failed to recognize Bill Abbot. 'Police. But who's this?' he turned to look at Thorne.

'I'm Detective-Superintendent George Thorne,' said the Superintendent.

'Say! That does sound important. And what can we do for you, Detective-Superintendent?'

'May we look around for a few minutes?' Thorne said.

'Of course. Be our guests. But if you're hoping to find a cache of cannabis, or something that fell off the back of a lorry, you're going to be out of luck.'

'Really?' Thorne pointed to an arrangement of curtain material which, rather badly displayed, had a 'Bargain— For Sale' notice on a large card in front of it. 'What about that?'

'What about it?' Peter asked aggressively, reacting to Thorne's guess. 'I bought it myself off a chap in the Oxford market, because I thought we needed a few cheaper goods in the Galleries. So if you're suggesting—'

'Forget it,' Thorne said.

Without further comment he made for the spiral staircase that led up to the gallery, and Peter followed him. He strolled around it, glancing at the paintings and prints and pieces of sculpture on display. Then he leant carefully on the waist-high railing, testing it, and judged the distance to the floor below. There was no doubt that anything heavy dropped from that height could have killed an unsuspecting person, but it would have been a chancy business, stupid in the extreme.

'Take care!' Peter said involuntarily and, as Thorne stared at him in simulated surprise, added, 'I'd hate to be blamed if you fell over, Detective-Superintendent.'

'Have you ever had an accident here?' Thorne asked, ignoring the slight sarcasm inherent in Peter Drayton's repetitive use of his full rank.

Peter replied without apparent hesitation. 'If you mean has anyone ever fallen over, no. But a few weeks ago my sister and I were fooling around a bit and we dropped a great bit of sculpture almost on top of my dad and my poor Aunt Helen and a local vicar, who were chatting away down there. Luckily there was no harm done, except to the sculpture.'

Thorne made no comment. He was thinking that Peter Drayton was either a fine actor, or he was innocent of any evil intent towards his aunt. On the other hand, he had been unnecessarily aggressive earlier in the interview.

Thoughtfully the Superintendent made his way down the stairs to the ground floor. Two men had appeared from a door in the rear of the shop, and were standing and talking. Thorne was glad to see that Abbot was placed so that he could hear what they were saying. Peter Drayton, however, also immediately realized this.

'Dad,' he called. 'I've a policeman here to see you. Detective-Superintendent Thorne.'

It was obvious to Thorne which of the two men was Paul Drayton. In spite of the fact that Paul looked bleak and ill, the resemblance to his son was strong. But both Drayton and his companion seemed equally startled by Peter's announcement. Their conversation ceased abruptly, and they regarded Thorne with a mixture of dislike and distrust.

Thorne sensed that behind his back Peter had given some encouraging gesture, because Paul Drayton suddenly relaxed and gave a weak smile. Thorne said, 'Good morning, Mr Drayton, Mr—?' He looked inquiringly at the other man.

'Slinter. Frank Slinter. But you won't be interested in me, Superintendent. I'm just a customer here.'

'Then I won't bother you at the moment, Mr Slinter. I'll call on you later in the day, or tomorrow, depending on how my inquiries progress.'

'What inquiries?' Slinter demanded, flushing angrily. 'I tell you there's no—'

'Inquiries into the death of Miss Helen Fayne.'

'But—but we all know how she died,' Paul Drayton protested, apparently surprised. 'She crashed her car into a stone wall.'

'After a party at the residence of Sir Reginald and Lady Clutton-Grey.' Thorne nodded his head in sympathy as he spoke. 'I know, Mr Drayton, and I expect it's stupid, a waste of the taxpayers' money. But a friend of hers feels that your sister-in-law has been maligned, that to suggest the series of accidents she'd recently suffered—and especially the fatal one—were due to alcohol is absurd, and that there must be some other explanation.'

Thorne paused, waiting for a comment, but neither the Draytons nor Frank Slinter seemed prepared to offer one. They appeared totally bemused by what the Superintendent has just said, and he was forced to ask them for their opinions.

'What do you think? Did Miss Fayne have too much to drink at that party?' He looked at each of them in turn, as if conducting a poll.

'No.' Paul Drayton said firmly, perhaps a shade too firmly. 'Helen never drank too much when she was driving. I remember thinking at the time of the inquest that it was wrong to suggest it. But what other explanation could there be, unless she suddenly felt faint or ill? I don't suppose we shall ever know,' he ended sadly.

'And don't ask me,' Slinter said. 'I scarcely spoke to the lady. Ask Reggie Clutton-Grey. He saw her out.'

'I intend to.' Thorne was terse.

'This—this friend you mentioned,' Peter said. 'Who was it, Superintendent?'

'I'm afraid I can't tell you that, Mr Drayton,' Thorne replied quickly. 'It's confidential information. But what about you? Did you think your aunt was drunk?'

'Drunk, no. But a bit upset, perhaps. After the food flew all over the place . . .'

As the Bands had not been at the Clutton-Greys' party, this was the first Thorne had heard of the mishap with the plate of canapés. He listened with what seemed to be polite interest, but asked no questions—to the surprise of Abbot who throughout the conversation had been standing silently by. And, almost immediately afterwards, Thorne looked at his watch and said they had an appointment.

'With a pint of beer and a good meal, I hope, Sergeant,' Thorne said as they left the Galleries and walked along the High Street to the Windrush Arms. 'It'll give the Draytons and friend Slinter a chance to spread the happy news of our "inquiries". Let's hope it worries someone very much.'

'From what I overheard, Slinter's paid off the debt he owed the Galleries,' Abbot said. 'That's what he was doing with Paul Drayton in the office at the back of the shop. So he only gained a few weeks by Helen Fayne's death, that's all. It doesn't seem to me a very adequate motive.'

'Maybe not,' Thorne said, 'but if it had become known that he was having trouble paying his debts all his creditors would have been on his back. Men have been ruined by less. Anyway, it's far too early to be reaching conclusions, though I must admit that, having viewed the scene, I'd be surprised if the sculpture incident was other than pure accident.'

The Windrush Arms was the most popular hotel and eating place in Colombury. The bar was crowded and the dining-room, tables closely packed, was already beginning to fill. However, the two police officers were shown to seats conveniently side by side in a corner of the room.

Thorne, having ordered their beer, said, 'Well, we get a good view of the proceedings from here, at least, Abbot.' He sat back, pleased, and surveyed the room, stroking his moustache.

Most of the clientele were men, locals who lunched there regularly, or farmers and growers in town for market day. Only three or four women were among them, but two of these—at a nearby table—were a somewhat surprising couple. They were both expensively and elegantly dressed, and they stood out from the crowd though they gave no sign of being aware of it. Engrossed in their conversation, they spoke in high and penetrating voices. It was impossible for anyone moderately close not to eavesdrop.

'—absolutely absurd of the girl,' the younger woman was saying irritably. 'The men will sell, of course. All they care about is the money.'

'I suppose she wants it for herself,' said the older one. 'That's why she's being so difficult.'

Abbot leant closer to Thorne. 'Those two females, sir. The black-and-white check—Kathleen—is the present Lady Clutton-Grey, and the green suit is Jean, Frank Slinter's wife.'

'Really?' Thorne, who had been concentrating on the menu, now gave them his attention. 'No one's told me they were such bosom friends.'

'I don't think they are, sir. I'm surprised to see them here together.'

The arrival of a waiter to take their orders caused an interruption, but when he had gone the two women resumed their talk, and their listeners continued to catch snatches of it. Inevitably, some was lost as the dining-room became more crowded, and the noise level increased. But what was heard was tantalizing.

'—could try a little pressure, my dear.'

'On the girl? Would she care?'

'Perhaps not, but her parents would. The Draytons are a churchy family, regular as clockwork every Sunday at St Augustine's.'

Thorne, who had been studying the two women, and only paying slight attention to their half-heard conversation, was immediately alert. He ignored what Abbot was muttering and strained to hear more clearly what was being said at the nearby table, cursing himself for not having realized earlier who they were talking about.

'—a sex scandal, my dear. Imagine it!' Jean Slinter laughed.

Lady Clutton-Grey's smile was scarcely sympathetic. 'In

this particular instance I find it extraordinarily difficult
to imagine,' she said coldly. She gave her companion a
contemptuous glance, but Mrs Slinter, intent on her thick
vegetable soup, failed to appreciate it. 'You're absolutely
positive about this, Jean? I must admit I did once make an
oblique reference to it, and—'

Thorne missed the rest of the sentence. A party of four men
had taken the adjacent table, and immediately commenced a
heated discussion about food mountains in the EEC. They
completely drowned the women, the more so because Jean
Slinter had moved closer to Lady Clutton-Grey and lowered
her voice to a confidential level.

'You heard that, Abbot?' Thorne said. 'A sex scandal—
in Colombury—well!'

Abbot shrugged. 'Depends what she meant, sir—and
who. Peter Drayton, perhaps? I wouldn't put anything past
him, if he had the chance. But give a dog a bad name
and—'

'And the reverse is true, too,' Thorne said, thinking that
there was some reference in Shakespeare, or was it the Bible
—Miranda would know—about a good name being beyond
price.

CHAPTER 13

After an excellent lunch, Superintendent Thorne suggested
that Sergeant Abbot should take him for a drive. They
passed the cottage where Susan and Andrew Hill lived
with Jeremy, went by the Draytons' house and skirted the
Clutton-Greys' estate. They stopped at the end of the lane
where Vain Glory had bolted, inspected the scene of the
fatal crash and took a circuitous route through Windfield
village to reach South Winds.

'At least that's given me some idea of the relation of one place to another,' said Thorne, as Abbot brought the car to a halt.

'Yes, sir. But remember the geography's not exactly as it appears,' Abbot warned. 'For instance, there's a path across the fields from the church to near South Winds, and it's possible to cut through the grounds of the Hall from the big house to the Faynes, though naturally the Clutton-Greys don't encourage that as a public right of way.'

Thorne grunted. 'At any rate we're in luck,' he said, nodding towards a Volvo parked outside South Winds. There's someone here. I wonder who. Let's go and see.'

The door was opened to them by Mrs Ferguson, who made no attempt to hide her surprise when the two visitors introduced themselves as police officers. But she let them into the hall without hesitation, and said she would fetch Mrs Drayton. While they waited they studied the staircase.

'Steep,' Thorne said. 'A nasty fall, especially for someone not too young.'

Abbot was bending down, examining the stair rods. 'I'd say these were professionally fixed, sir, and they're pretty firm. Unless it was already loosened, Miss Fayne must have been unlucky to catch her slipper in one.'

He straightened himself hurriedly as Biddy appeared on the landing above, followed by Mrs Ferguson, but there was no doubt that the women had seen what he was doing. Biddy made no comment. Mrs Ferguson, however, had grown red-faced, and was bristling with indignation.

'You've not come about Miss Fayne's fall, I hope,' she said. 'Because if you have I'll tell you straight out what I told everyone at the time. I cleaned those stairs the morning before, and those rods were fine when I left them. I'm always most particular about that.'

'Don't be silly, Mrs Ferguson,' said Bridget Drayton firmly. 'No one's ever blamed you for that accident, and anyway I'm sure these police officers have more important things to concern them than poor Helen falling downstairs.' She smiled at Thorne. 'Come along in here, Superintendent, Sergeant.'

As Thorne followed her into the sitting-room, he felt that his plot—if you could call it that—was already working as he planned. The news of his inquiries had begun to spread. Mrs Ferguson had obviously not been expecting them, but it was almost inconceivable that Mrs Drayton hadn't been warned; either Paul or Peter would have phoned her.

'Do sit down,' Biddy said, waving them to chairs. 'I'm sorry the place is in something of a mess, but I'm in the middle of sorting out my late sister's effects—with Mrs Ferguson's help.' She paused, then went on. 'Mrs Ferguson really does blame herself for that fall, you know, and of course she's probably right. Even the most careful people can make mistakes.'

Thorne nodded his agreement. 'Perhaps that's why Miss Fayne had her final accident—the fatal one,' he said. 'She just made a mistake. Or do you believe she'd had too much to drink, Mrs Drayton?' He looked pointedly at the array of bottles and glasses on a side-table, and wondered idly if they were always kept on view in this way, or had been displayed for his benefit.

'Personally I believe it was a combination of several things, Superintendent. Helen had certainly been drinking; after all, it was a party. But she'd got a good head, and she was used to liquor.' Biddy made a small gesture towards the side-table. 'She entertained quite a lot, mostly for our mother's sake. Our mother was arthritic and didn't get out much, so . . .'

Thorne let her talk until, with a deprecating laugh, she said, 'But you can't be interested in all this idiotic family gossip, Superintendent. I'm as bad as Mrs Ferguson. Tell me why you're really here.'

'It's fairly obvious, Mrs Drayton. I'm making inquiries concerning Miss Fayne's death,' Thorne said bluntly.

'But—I don't understand . . .'

Thorne repeated his tale about the friend who thought that Helen Fayne's reputation had been maligned. Immediately Biddy asked the identity of the friend, but Thorne merely shook his head.

'I can guess,' Biddy said. 'It was Tim Merle, wasn't it? Stupid fool!' she added when Thorne didn't deny it. 'What does it matter now? My poor sister's dead, and that's that.' She shook her head in exasperation. 'A waste of time and effort, Superintendent. I'd have thought the police had better things to do.'

'Our informant—er—has friends in high places, I gather, and was able to pull some strings. So please bear with me, Mrs Drayton. It's not my fault I'm here.'

Abbot, who had taken no part in the conversation, had trouble in hiding his amusement at Thorne's last remark. He hoped that Biddy Drayton would find a meek, apologetic Superintendent more convincing than he did. Evidently she took the bait, because at once she nodded her understanding.

'Yes. I'd heard a rumour about Merle's family, but I didn't know if it was true. He never talks of his relations.'

Thorne stroked his moustache hard. He had no idea what Biddy meant. Nor did he propose to divert the interview by asking her. Instead, he reminded her that she had earlier commented that Helen's car crash might have been due to a variety of causes.

'Yes,' Biddy replied. 'Well, as we know, she *had* been drinking. No one can deny that. Perhaps there was a moment's carelessness, though she was an excellent driver and she knew the turning out of the drive like the back of her hand.'

She hesitated for a moment. Then finally she said, 'I might as well be frank. My sister had all the brains in the family, but she wasn't terribly attractive—she was the last person who should have been called Helen. Anyway, I suppose it was because of this that she was both aggressive and shy, rather like my son, Gavin. In fact, she lacked genuine poise. And at that party her composure wasn't improved by Tim Merle knocking a plate of canapés over her. Wretched man!' Biddy sighed. 'I can't imagine why he's trying to make a mystery out of what was a simple sad happening.'

Again Thorne didn't correct Mrs Drayton's misapprehension. He got to his feet, apologized for taking up her time, somewhat belatedly offered his condolences and indicated to Abbot that they should go. In the car, he said, 'If that doesn't help the stew to bubble, I'll be surprised.'

Abbot looked at his superior askance. 'Where to now, sir? To the vicar's? To warn him the news will soon get around that he's responsible for these unexpected police inquiries? Let's hope no one attempts to get rid of him as a result.'

'Why on earth should they?' asked Thorne. 'He's been to the police. He's told them all he knows. Surely he's the last person to be a threat. No, we won't warn him, Abbot, but we'll certainly go and have a chat with him.'

The Reverend Timothy Merle, however, was nowhere to be found. He was neither in his cottage nor in the church. Time was passing, and Thorne had begun to think with pleasant anticipation of afternoon tea. He decided that their best bet was probably Susan Hill, and anyway this was a call that had to be made.

At the Hills' house they were lucky. Susan was in her sitting-room, having just completed a pile of ironing. 'The kitchen's so small, it's impossible to iron there,' she said rather bitterly by way of apology, 'and I always have so much. Jeremy's got some kind of allergy and he has to wear natural fibres—none of this drip-dry stuff.' She bustled around the room, attempting to tidy it, or at least make room for the visitors to sit. Abbot put down the ironing board for her, and carried it into the kitchen. He gave her his most appealing smile.

'If you show me where things are, Mrs Hill, I'll make us all a cup of tea while you talk to the Superintendent. We could do with one, and I'm sure you could too.'

'All right.' Quickly Susan produced a box of teabags, milk and sugar, and opened the cupboard where the crockery was kept. 'Use those cups and saucers,' she said. 'Biscuits in that tin. And there's some cake in the other one.'

'Okay,' said Abbot cheerfully.

Susan left him to his task and went back to the sitting-room to join Thorne. She made no pretence of not knowing why the two police officers had called on her, but said immediately, 'It's about Aunt Helen, isn't it? Peter, my brother, phoned.'

'Yes,' Thorne said.

Susan's eyes filled with tears as she gave her account of the Clutton-Greys' party and her aunt's behaviour. Thorne listened silently and sympathetically. 'You were fond of your aunt?' he said when she paused.

'Yes, I was. I've only just begun to realize how much I loved her. I know people make jokes about spinster aunts, and Aunt Helen did have her funny little ways. She could be annoying, too. But really she was very generous to all of us—especially to Jeremy, my son. She went to endless trouble over his birthday parties.'

Susan gulped loudly, and Thorne was afraid she might be about to cry. Luckily at that moment Abbot brought in the tea, and the diversion gave Susan an opportunity to regain control of her emotions. She poured, passed the biscuits, cut the cake. Suddenly she laughed.

'I've never had tea with two policemen before,' she said.

'We're quite human,' Abbot said, and hurriedly

swallowed the words he had been going to add.

Thorne added them for him. 'At least some of us are, Mrs Hill. Incidentally, I should have asked you before. How is Jeremy? I think it was your mother who said he was ill after his latest birthday party,' he lied.

'Oh, you've already seen Mother, have you? I don't understand—' She frowned in perplexity, and then returned to Thorne's question. 'You were asking about Jeremy. He's fine now, thank you. The doctor said it was probably just some tainted food, but it was ghastly at the time. I was afraid he was going to die. Luckily none of the other little guests were affected.' She glanced at her watch. 'Jeremy'll be home soon. A friend's fetching him from school today. We take it in turns.'

Thorne nodded. He wasn't interested. He had no wish to see the child. 'To return to your Aunt Helen,' he said. 'What's your opinion, Mrs Hill? Do you believe she'd had too much to drink, and that's why she drove into the wall.'

'No, I don't. And I think it's horrible of anyone to suggest it. It was a pure accident.'

'Like her fall downstairs and her adventure with her horse?'

Susan Hill stared at the Superintendent, her mouth slightly open. 'Why not?' she said at last. 'Things go in threes, don't they?'

It was a weak comment, Thorne thought, but he responded. 'Sometimes,' he said. 'Sometimes. Well, thank you for the tea, Mrs Hill. We must be off to our next appointment.'

Thorne said goodbye at the front door with unusual heartiness, and Abbot followed his example. Susan stood on the doorstep watching them depart.

As they drove away Abbot noticed that Thorne was smiling to himself. He ventured. 'She'll be on the phone to her husband and her ma and the rest of them in a minute, sir.'

'Let's hope so. What did you think of the house, Sergeant? A nice little place, but very small. South Winds would be much better for them.'

Abbot was genuinely shocked. 'Sir, you're not suggesting that that girl might have . . .' He shook his head in disbelief. 'Where now, sir?' he asked at last.

'Let's try the Derwent Stables,' replied Thorne. I've had enough of the Drayton clan for the moment.'

Lorna Castle had gone to a gymkhana organized by the local pony club where some of her pupils were performing and had not yet returned, but her husband was in the tack room. David Castle had been an officer in the Guards until he lost a leg and half a lung in the Falklands. That he had chosen not to die, but to make the best of what was left to him was largely due to his wife. The two police officers found a man in his middle thirties, outgoing, intelligent and with a sense of humour.

'Detective-Superintendent?' he said. 'This must be important. Better come along to the office.'

The office was small and next door to the tack room. It boasted a desk with a computer terminal, a couple of filing cabinets and two hard chairs. Castle gestured to the chairs, and himself perched on the end of the desk. 'Now,' he said, 'how can I help you?'

'It concerns Miss Helen Fayne,' Thorpe began, and paused for a reaction.

'Does it now? I had an idea it might. Poor dear! She was such a pleasant, kind individual. No beauty, unfortunately. And certainly no horsewoman, though she wasn't scared of the beasts.' David Castle smiled sadly. 'She had neither seat nor hands, but she enjoyed her weekly hack, and she had no pretensions—not like some. She was far too bright not to know her own limitations.'

While Castle talked the Superintendent had been summing him up, and had decided that here was one man he could trust. After all, if anything, the Castles had lost rather than gained by Helen Fayne's death. A different approach was needed here. Obfuscation would be pointless.

'Major Castle, may I rely—'

'*Mr* Castle, please. I don't use my rank.'

Thorne nodded, accepting the correction, and liking Castle the more for it. 'May I rely on you to treat what I'm about to tell you in confidence?'

'If you'll let me tell my wife, yes, of course. Whatever it is, it won't go further than us, I can promise you that.'

'Thank you.' Thorne bowed his head in acknowledgement. 'The point is that recently Miss Fayne seems to have become accident prone, as they say. Two theories for this have been advanced, one that she was drinking too much, and as a result had grown careless, the other that the so-called accidents were deliberately engineered.'

Castle gave a low whistle. 'But who would want—' He stopped himself. 'I mustn't ask you that, I suppose.' He thought for a moment, and then continued. 'As far as that evening at the Clutton-Greys' is concerned, we left before she did, so I've no idea how she was when she drove off. But I can assure you she was perfectly sober when she spoke to us earlier. As for other accidents, I take it our mare bolting is one of them?'

'Yes,' said Thorne. 'I'm told Vain Glory—that's her name, isn't it?—is a gentle beast as a rule.'

'An old armchair. Myself, I didn't see Miss Fayne ride out that morning. The Slinters had just arrived, and—'

'Do they ride?' Thorne asked as if he found the idea somewhat surprising.

'Mrs Slinter's started having lessons recently, and sometimes her husband comes to watch. I know they were both here that day, because they kindly drove me over to the Clutton-Greys to collect Vain Glory after the incident. Anyway, as I say, I didn't see Miss Fayne ride out, but Lorna, my wife, said she was fine. We've never seen her otherwise.'

'You examined the horse when you got it back?'

'Naturally, and there was a puncture mark on her left rump. It was very small, but it had bled a little, though by the time I saw the mare the blood had congealed.'

'An insect bite? A bee, perhaps?'

'Not a bee. A bee will usually leave its sting behind, and I saw no sign of one. There was no inflammation either. I don't know what to suggest.'

'A dart?'

Castle gave the Superintendent a long look. 'I suspect you know more than you've told me.' he said.

Thorne explained that Helen had claimed to have found a dart at the place where Vain Glory had bucked and bolted, and Castle agreed that it might have been the cause of the mare's behaviour. Further than that, he wouldn't commit himself. Then Lorna returned, proud of the several rosettes her pupils had won. But she could add nothing to her husband's remarks, except to comment that a good horsewoman should have been able to regain control of Vain Glory before she reached the road.

'Frankly, I was surprised Miss Fayne managed to stay on at all,' she said. 'I'd have expected her to fall just as soon as Vain Glory bucked. Luck, I suppose. Or quick thinking.'

Thorne and Abbot drove back to Oxford, intending to interview Gavin Drayton. They had been told he lived in a so-called 'garden flat' off the Woodstock Road, but when they found the place and identified the right door, it looked more like the basement of a typical North Oxford red-brick house, set back from the street behind a surprisingly tidy front garden with a gravel drive.

But their journey was fruitless. They descended stone steps and tried the bell, but there was no answer to their repeated rings. Abbot suggested they might make inquiries from other tenants, but Thorne thought of the paperwork that would have accumulated on his desk.

'We're not far from Kidlington,' the Superintendent said, 'so we'll call it a day. At least it's not been entirely wasted.'

'I suppose not, sir,' said Abbot doubtfully. 'Though I'm beginning to wonder if there's a case at all. All these supposed attempts on Miss Fayne have been so—so hit or miss.'

'I agree,' said Thorne. 'Unless they were meant as warnings of some kind. Perhaps even the last one was meant as a warning, but it succeeded only too well. Cheer up, Sergeant. Tomorrow's another day, and maybe we'll strike lucky.'

'Yes, sir,' said Abbot, and thought that tomorrow was Saturday. It would have been fine to have the day free, like so many of his friends.

CHAPTER 14

At nine o'clock the next morning Detective-Superintendent Thorne and Detective-Sergeant Abbot arrived once more at Gavin Drayton's flat in North Oxford. Once again they parked in the gravel drive, descended the steps and rang the bell. And again, there was no answer.

'He could be away, sir,' Abbot remarked. 'Or at work.'

'I checked before we left,' said Thorne impatiently. 'He never works on Saturdays. More likely to be sleeping off a heavy night. Try again, Sergeant. Lean on the ruddy bell.'

The Superintendent was right. After a couple more minutes Abbot's efforts were rewarded and the door was opened by a surly Gavin Drayton in dressing-gown and slippers. His hair was ruffled, his eyes bloodshot, his skin blotchy with sleep. He was not an attractive figure.

'What the hell do you want?' he demanded.

'Police!' Thorne said succinctly, producing his warrant card.

Gavin didn't bother to look at it. 'Oh yes! My brother warned me you might be appearing. Some nonsense about my aunt—Okay. I suppose you'd better come in.'

He led them along a passage, past a couple of closed doors, and into a large rectangular room. In spite of the unmade divan bed, the papers strewn over the desk and piles of clothes and books in odd corners, it was a pleasant room. In this case, the term 'garden flat' was not a euphemism. At the back of the house the basement was at ground level, and long windows looked out over a well-kept lawn surrounded by pleasant shrubs. The general impression was of brightness and space.

But what immediately attracted the attention of the two police officers was the darts board in the middle of the far wall. At a nod from Thorne, Abbot strolled over to examine it. Without asking permission he opened the two boxes of darts stacked on a table beneath the board.

'What on earth are you doing?' Gavin Drayton, who had been clearing two chairs for his unwelcome guests, had just noticed Abbot's behaviour.

'Keen on darts, are you?' Abbot asked, as he moved back to the Superintendent and said very quietly, 'Both boxes full. Three in each.'

Gavin Drayton showed his surprise at the Sergeant's question. 'Moderately, I suppose,' he said. 'I play in the pub, but I don't have a great deal of time for it.' He sat suddenly on the divan. 'I thought you'd come about Aunt Helen What the hell have my darts got to do with you?'

'We'll ask the questions, Mr Drayton,' Thorne said carefully. 'Now, before her death Miss Fayne seems to have become—accident prone, shall we say?—as a result of drinking to excess. Would you agree with that comment, Mr Drayton?'

'I don't see that it matters a damn, but for what my opinion's worth, no. I don't agree. She wasn't a drunk. Not that I'd have blamed her if she had been.'

'Why not?' asked Thorne at once.

'Well, she didn't have much of a life, did she? Looking after Gran—and Gran could be a trial sometimes. Running the Galleries for my incompetent father. Bullied by my mother, and used by all the family—me included. Then by the time she's free of Gran and might have begun to enjoy herself, she's in her mid-fifties, and it's really too late.'

Drayton spoke with the confidence of youth, but Thorne, for whom the fifties were not so far away, looked somewhat askance at this remark. He said abruptly, 'You realize you'll inherit a tidy sum, don't you?'

'I sincerely hope so.' Gavin Drayton, having paid tribute to his late aunt, seemed prepared to be frank. 'It all depends on what happens to South Winds. The Clutton-Greys will pay twice what it's worth, but at the moment my sister, Susan, refuses to agree to sell to them. She wants to buy out Peter and me at the ordinary going rate, and live in the place with her family. Peter doesn't mind. To him it looks like a fortune either way, but I want to start my own computer business, and the more I can get the better.'

'Even at a valuation figure, with your share from the Galleries, I should have thought—' Thorne began.

Gavin interrupted. 'We don't get anything from the Galleries, none of us. That all goes to Dad. When Aunt Helen became a partner they made an agreement saying that when one of them died, the other would inherit the whole business.'

'I see,' said Thorne thoughtfully. 'That's not a very usual arrangement.'

'Perhaps not, but there it is.' Suddenly Gavin Drayton perceived the direction in which the Superintendent's questions had been pointing. He ran his fingers through his rumpled hair, and glared at Thorne. 'Now look here,' he said, 'if you're suggesting my father or any of the family had anything to do with Aunt Helen's death you should do your homework—read your own bloody files. She killed herself. Maybe she was a bit tight. Maybe she wasn't. What the hell does it matter? Why don't you tell that old parson to stuff it, instead of wasting my time and yours?'

Angry, Gavin Drayton jumped to his feet. Thorne rose more slowly, followed by Abbot. Without a word, Gavin marched ahead of them and opened the front door. The Superintendent thanked him for his help.

'What help?' Drayton demanded.

Thorne merely smiled. 'Just one more point, Mr Drayton. We can check, of course, but it would save time and effort if you told us. Your dartboard looks well-used, but when and where did you last buy any darts for it?'

'Darts? You're still on to darts!' Gavin's voice was harsh with disbelief. 'I thought you were nuts before; now I'm sure.'

'Kindly answer the Superintendent's question, Mr Drayton,' Abbot said sharply.

Gavin shook his shaggy head. 'Why shouldn't I? I haven't bought any for myself for ages. But a couple of months ago I bought a cheap board and a box of darts at that toy shop near Carfax down in Oxford. I gave them to my sister for young Jeremy. I thought it might entertain him to play, but Susan said they were too dangerous. I've no idea where they are now.'

Thorne thanked him again, and the two detectives departed. 'The stew thickens,' Thorne said with satisfaction. 'Let's go in search of those darts, Abbot.'

At the Hills' house they found Susan with her brother, Peter. Jeremy, she said, had gone to visit a young friend, and her husband was at the school. Andrew often worked on Saturdays in term-time, giving extra coaching or supervising various activities.

'Such as darts?' Abbot asked with a grin.

'Darts? Why darts? What the hell have darts got to do with it?' Unconsciously Peter echoed his brother's reaction.

Sergeant Abbot's response was unexpected. 'Better darts than drugs,' he said.

As he admitted to his Superintendent later, it was the first comment that came into his head, perhaps because the use of drugs at boarding schools had been in the news recently. He had absolutely no ulterior motive in using the words, except that they seemed to juxtapose themselves pleasantly. But Paul Drayton immediately took offence.

'If you're thinking of trying to pin any drugs charges on me, you can think again,' he said belligerently.

'There's no question of that,' Thorne assured him mildly.

'And you won't find any in this house either.' It wasn't obvious whether Susan was leaping to her brother's defence, or making her own position clear. 'Neither drugs—nor darts.'

'Oh yes, these darts. They're what we're trying to trace.' Thorne noted the exchange of questioning glances between brother and sister; but he also registered the fact that seemingly Gavin Drayton hadn't bothered to warn them of the unusual interest the police were taking in darts. 'Mr Gavin Drayton intended a darts board and a box of darts as a present for young Jeremy, I gather, but you considered him too young for the game.'

'That's right, yes,' Susan said, surprised. 'You want to

trace them—the board and the darts? Why? Anyway, I've no idea where they are now. They were in Jeremy's cupboard for a while, though I forbade him to play with them. Then eventually my husband took them up to Coriston College for the boys in his House.'

'I see. Thank you. Thank you very much,' said Thorne.

'Why thank me? And why should you care about those darts?' Susan asked again.

'Perhaps someone threw one at Aunt Helen and made her drive into the wall,' Peter said sarcastically.

'That's an idea, Mr Drayton. I must consider it.' Thorne nodded at Susan. 'Goodbye for the present, Mrs Hill.'

Abbot smiled at her, and gave Peter Drayton what he hoped was an enigmatic stare before following his superior out of the house. In the car, directed to drive to Coriston College, he was flattered when the Superintendent asked his opinion of Gavin, Peter and Susan—the main beneficiaries from Helen Fayne's death.

'To be honest, sir, I can't really see any of them in the role of villain. I think that if Gavin had decided to get rid of his aunt, or anyone else for that matter, he'd have made a much more efficient job of it. Peter—I just can't see it; I can't imagine that chap going to all that effort. Incidentally, he was a bit touchy about drugs, don't you think? We might get the Drugs Squad to check if they've ever come across him.'

'I agree,' said Thorne. 'Look after it.'

'As for Susan,' Abbot continued. 'No—though it's only a guess. But what about the older Draytons? I know they're pretty well off, but no one has too much money and if Paul gets Helen's share of the Galleries he could sell the business. I doubt if he could make a go of it by himself—as far as I can see, it was Helen Fayne who was the brains behind the business. And I'd be surprised if Peter'll be prepared to stay on here now. He'll be off to London as soon as he gets his share of the estate. So, I'd say Paul's the best possibility to date, sir.'

'M—mm,' Thorne mused. 'To date, perhaps. But we've still got the Clutton-Greys and the vicar to consider. And we've not met Andrew Hill yet.'

They drove through the gates of Coriston College, and stopped the first boy they came across on the drive. He at once volunteered to take them to Nelson House, where he said Mr Hill would be found. He got in the car to direct them up the long drive, and stared at the complex radio equipment under the dashboard.

'Police?' the boy asked suddenly.

Thorne hesitated. The car was unmarked, but the boy was obviously bright. 'Yes,' he said, 'but we're only making a routine inquiry.'

'I see,' said the boy doubtfully.

When they reached Nelson House, they found that Andrew Hill was not in the small room which, as assistant house master, he used as a study. The boy said he would go and find him, and left the police officers there.

Thorne wandered around the room, coming to rest in front of a large chart on the wall. He glanced at it idly, then realized that it was an extremely elaborate time-table, resplendent with multi-coloured inks. He was studying it when the boy returned to say that Mr Hill would be with them in a few minutes.

'Half a second,' he said as the boy was about to leave. 'Come and tell me about this chart.'

'It's a time-table for masters, sir. It shows you where they are and what they're doing at any hour of the day.' He was slightly overawed by Thorne, but he grinned. 'Or where they ought to be. Sometimes they swap duties.'

'Look at that Saturday,' Thorne pointed. 'According to the way I read it, I'd say your Mr Hill was here all the morning, supervising something called 'EP'. Is that right?'

The boy nodded. 'Yes, sir, that's right. Extra prep. You get it either for poor work, or sometimes as a punishment —detention you could call it. And Mr Hill *was* there, too, because so was I. It was the first detention I've had this term, so I remember.'

'Thank you,' Thorne said solemnly, and drew a deep breath. He wasn't particularly good with children, he knew, but this boy had been most responsive.

Then the boy said suddenly. 'Does that mean that Mr Hill's in the clear, sir? He didn't do it?'

Before Thorne could answer the door of the study swung open, and a big man, black gown billowing around him, mortar board on his head, strode into the little room. He seized the boy by the shoulders, turned him round and ran him out of the door. Then he slammed it shut after him.

'I should like to do the same to both of you,' he said aggressively.

Andrew Hill was large in every sense, and muscular. He looked like the rugger full-back that until recently he had been. He towered over Superintendent Thorne, and made Sergeant Abbot look medium-sized. The cap and gown added to his alarming appearance. He glared at his unwelcome visitors.

'Why come here to the school?' he demanded. 'And tell that damned boy you're policemen. Don't you understand what a place like this is like? In a few hours—minutes— it'll be all over the school that the police have come to interview me or arrest me, or hang me or something. You ought to have more bloody sense.'

'Our car's unmarked, and we didn't tell him,' Thorne said mildly. 'But he seems to be a bright lad and he guessed. We're sorry if it embarrasses you.' Thorne paused, then continued with a straight face. 'But we don't have to talk here, you know. If you'd prefer to come to our Headquarters in Kidlington instead, we'd have no objection, Mr Hill.'

Abbot, who knew this was merely a ploy on the Superintendent's part, smothered with a cough his desire to smirk. He had never yet seen George Thorne intimidated by anyone; nor did he expect he ever would. And, as he had anticipated, Andrew Hill lost most of his aggressiveness at once.

'For God's sake,' he said with ill grace, flinging his mortar board into a corner of the room, 'that'd merely make it worse. And I haven't got time to go traipsing all over the countryside. Anyway, I suppose the damage is done now. You might as well stay, and conduct your inquiries, or whatever you call it.'

'In that case perhaps we should introduce ourselves,' Thorne said, and did so.

'Right. Sit down then.' Hill seemed more composed now, and indicated a couple of hard chairs. 'I assume all this is connected with my wife's Aunt Helen. That fool of a parson's been making trouble, I gather.'

'A few questions,' murmured Thorne.

In spite of his obvious distaste for the situation, Andrew Hill answered Thorne's questions with studied care. Apart from an occasional shake of the head to imply that the queries were incomprehensible to him, he didn't actually query their relevance in any way. On the surface his aggressiveness seemed to have given way to boredom.

He agreed that he had brought the darts board and the box of darts to the school and given them to the boys. He offered to try to find them, though he pointed out that those particular darts would almost certainly have been mixed up with others by now. 'Boys don't keep things all that tidily, you know,' he said.

'You don't remember how many darts were in the box, by any chance?' Thorne asked casually.

Hill stared at him. 'How did you know? I do remember

noticing there were two instead of three. I asked Jeremy where the other one was, and he admitted he'd been playing with them in spite of his mother's instructions, but didn't know he'd lost one. However, surely this is trivial. What's the point?'

'Just clearing up loose ends,' said Thorne. 'Now, let's move to something of more obvious importance—the fatal crash. Do you have any views on that?'

Hill gave it as his opinion that Helen Fayne had been 'a bit tight' at the Clutton-Greys' party, but not enough to cause any comment. He said that she took antacid tablets for mild but chronic indigestion, but as far as he knew no other drugs. He admitted that there had been a little trouble over drugs—mostly amphetamines—at the school the previous year and shook his head resignedly. He was not unco-operative, but Thorne learnt little from him.

'Well, I suppose we know that Andrew Hill has an alibi for that Saturday morning, and couldn't have made Vain Glory bolt, but that's about all,' the Superintendent remarked as they left Coriston College. 'I'm beginning to wonder if you're not right, Sergeant. Maybe there never was an actual crime.'

CHAPTER 15

Sergeant Abbot's judgement had been poor. The pub he chose for lunch had changed hands since he had last patronized it, and it was partly because of the indifferent food that George Thorne felt depression settling over him. The case, too, was depressing. The Superintendent was well aware that most detection involved a good deal of dull, methodical slogging, often with no result. But usually there was some end in view, a crime to be solved, and very often the villain could be identified fairly readily, even though he or she might never be brought to justice becaused of lack of such evidence as would satisfy the DPP's office.

But this case—if it could be called a case—was quite different. The word for it, Thorne ruminated, was insubstantial. In spite of his best efforts, he had been unable to find any concrete evidence to support Helen Fayne's claim that someone had wanted her dead. True, she had convinced the Bands, the Bands had in turn originally convinced him, and the Chief Constable had respected his opinion. But time was running short. Thorne knew that unless he could soon come up with some justification—some evidence—Philip Midvale would have no alternative but to order him to discontinue his inquiries.

'We'll try the Clutton-Greys,' he said to Abbot gloomily. 'After all, Sir Reginald seems to have been the last person to speak to Helen Fayne.'

They turned into the Hall's drive and stopped twenty yards inside the open gates. They got out of their car and walked back to survey once again the stone wall into which Helen had driven. Once again they examined the angle at which she had hit the wall, and the remains of the damage that had been done. They had, of course, both studied the reports on the accident, and knew there had been no skid marks, and no other sign that the driver had made any attempt to brake, or indeed to make the turn into the road. The driver had been much more than merely careless, and at least on the surface the incident was a clear-cut and flagrant example of drunken driving. Yet no one had been found to state categorically that Helen Fayne had been drunk when she left the Hall.

'Definitely not,' said Reginald Clutton-Grey. 'If I'd believed that I wouldn't have allowed her to drive away. I remember noting at one point—I think it was by the front door—that she was perhaps a trifle unsteady. She drove

away pretty sharply, abruptly, you know what I mean—
wheels spinning on the gravel and all that. And of course,
as I'm sure you know already, she forgot to fasten her
seat-belt. But she only had a short way to go on a country
road.'

'My husband feels guilty about the accident,' Kathleen
Clutton-Grey put in with an apologetic smile, 'though he
really has no need.'

'She was a nice woman,' Clutton-Grey remarked. 'Obstinate, like old Muriel, her mother, but basically much more
pleasant. I expect you've learnt now that neither of them
could be persuaded to sell me South Winds, Superintendent,
though I offered them a ludicrous price for the house.'

'Doubtless you'll be able to buy it now, sir.'

'I'm not so sure about that, unfortunately. The niece,
Susan, wants it for herself, and she seems to have inherited
the family's obstinacy.'

'Perhaps a little pressure could be applied,' Thorne said.

He looked directly at Kathleen Clutton-Grey, but she met
his gaze with apparent aplomb and made no comment on
his remark. Nevertheless, Thorne felt fairly sure that she
had recognized him as a neighbour at lunch at the Windrush
Arms the previous day, and he hoped she was wondering
how much of her conversation with Jean Slinter had been
overheard.

Her husband said, 'The only pressure I can think of is
more money. That might influence her, I suppose, but there
are limits.'

'You know South Winds, sir,' said Thorne. 'Can you tell
me if Miss Fayne always had a side-table in her sitting-room
well stocked with liquor?'

Clutton-Grey frowned. 'The last time I was there—actually I was inviting her to our party—the room was all
prepared for her nephew's birthday. But yes, I do remember.
She usually had a good supply of bottles.'

Thorne nodded. 'Thank you, sir. I think that's all for the present. I'm sorry to have bothered you.'

'It's no bother at all, Susperintendent. Though I must admit I can't imagine what our tame vicar hopes to achieve by making this fuss.'

Thorne looked shocked. He pulled at his moustache as if embarrassed. 'Sir Reginald, never have I mentioned the Reverend Timothy Merle's name in that context,' he said solemnly. 'May I ask where you got this information—this idea?' he corrected himself quickly.

Clutton-Grey gave a booming laugh. 'In the village post office,' he said. 'Mrs Beale, the postmistress, is a mine of information. What she doesn't know, old Nurse Whittaker does, and all they do is gossip. I'd be prepared to bet that by now there isn't a soul within a radius of ten miles who doesn't know about your inquiries, and who instigated them.'

Sir Reginald Clutton-Grey would have lost his bet. There was one person, much less than ten miles away, who was completely unaware of what was happening. That person was, of course, the Reverend Timothy Merle himself. He opened the door of his small house, and regarded the two police officers inquiringly.

'Good afternoon. What can I do for you?'

Thorne explained who they were. Merle looked surprised, but nodded and motioned them to follow him into the sitting-room. It was the Superintendent's turn to be surprised, for the room, though untidy, was comfortable, with a good carpet and curtains and well made, modern furniture. It was definitely a man's room, but someone with knowledge and taste—Thorne thought at once of Helen Fayne—had made it extremely pleasant.

Merle turned to face them. 'I can guess what you've come about,' he said.

'Exactly, sir. A friend is worried about what's happened here in Windfield, the perhaps surprising death . . .'

It was now that Merle interrupted Thorne to give the Superintendent his second surprise. 'I thought he might be. It's been preying on my mind, too. This friend—it's Dr Band, isn't it?' Merle said.

'What makes you think that?' asked Thorne.

'Because he was angry with me at the time. He thought I was incompetent and inefficient, and so I was. But she was dead. I'm not making excuses. There was no doubt she—'

'Dr Band was in Scotland.'

'Scotland? No!'

Abbot intervened. 'Sir, I think the Reverend Merle is talking about *Mrs* Fayne.'

'Yes, of course I am.' Merle nodded vigorously. 'Mrs Fayne. Muriel. Who else? There was clearly nothing anyone could have done for poor, dear Helen. No one could suggest it for a moment.'

The Superintendent took a deep breath. 'Perhaps we'd better start again, Mr Merle. Tell us about Muriel first.'

'She'd asked me to tea. I was nervous, I remember, because I was going to ask her for money. Not for myself, you understand, but for the church, and—'

As he talked it was obvious that Timothy Merle was re-living his experience of pulling Muriel Fayne from the lily-pond. His long thin hands clenched and unclenched nervously, and beads of sweat glistened on his upper lip. Occasionally he sighed deeply as if he felt a need to draw breath.

'—I should have given her the kiss of life, I know, but I —I couldn't. I kept on seeing—' He broke down and buried his face in his hands.

Abbot found his way to the kitchen and fetched a glass of water. He muttered to Thorne that he had put on the kettle

to make some tea. They sat in silence, waiting for Timothy
Merle to recover his composure. The whistle of the kettle
roused him.

'You're making tea for me—for us? Thank you. You're
very kind. I haven't always found the police so kind.' He
smiled somewhat wryly.

'Perhaps you'd tell us,' Thorne prompted gently.

'Yes, I will. It happened some years ago. I had a friend,
a dear friend—'

It was a sad story. Timothy Merle had taken the friend
to stay with his elder brother in the family home where they
had both been born, but the brother had made it perfectly
clear that the friend was not an acceptable guest in what
was now his house. As a result, Timothy and the friend had
quarrelled bitterly. The next morning the friend had been
found face down in the swimming-pool.

'The police suspected—suggested even—that I'd killed
him,' Merle said, 'but it was the last thing I'd have done. I
—I loved him. I didn't mind that he had a—a rather
dreadful accent, and didn't hold his knife and fork properly
and stupid, unimportant points like that. Dear God, when
I got him out of that pool and realized he was dead, I wished
it had been me.'

'Where did all this take place, sir?' Thorne inquired.

Merle hesitated. 'Does it matter?'

'Please, sir. Just for our own information.'

'In the North—er—the outskirts of Leeds, in fact.'

'And were you a clergyman then, sir?' Thorne asked as
Merle fell silent.

'Oh yes. And of course my bishop heard about it. It was
a minor scandal, though the—what shall I say?—the most
scandalous aspect in the eyes of the world was hushed up
when the police finally decided it was suicide. But I was
transferred here, to St Augustine's, which it's difficult not
to think of as a kind of dead-end job. Oh, I like the place,

so I suppose I should consider myself fortunate. But it's not the same as a city parish.'

Merle made a hopeless gesture. 'I don't know why I've told you all this, Superintendent, except to explain why I was so hopeless in dealing with Muriel Fayne. Perhaps if she'd not been wearing a blue dress—you see my friend was wearing blue, too, a blue dressing-gown, and—and—'

'Please don't upset yourself again, sir,' Thorne changed the subject quickly. 'Tell us about Miss Helen Fayne.'

'What do you want to know? She was a good, kind woman, a regular churchgoer. And she was intelligent. It may sound odd to you now, but we had quite a lot in common. I shall miss her, and not just because of the meals she was always giving me.' Merle smiled reminiscently. 'She'd asked me to supper the evening she died. That's why I was following her down the Clutton-Greys' drive. I'd come to the party on my bicycle and—'

'Yes, I understand,' Thorne said. 'Mr Merle, you were behind her. How did she drive? Was she—the worse for drink, shall we say?'

Merle hesitated. Then he said, 'Superintendent, Helen Fayne was never "the worse for drink".' Once again he seemed about to be overcome by his emotions.

George Thorne suppressed a sigh. 'Yes, sir. Tell me about the little contretemps with the canapés.'

'Oh, that was my stupidity again. I'd gone to get Miss Fayne a drink, and when I returned I was clumsy. I had the whisky in one hand and the plate in the other. Somehow I upset the lot.'

'The whisky, too?'

It was not an unimportant question, though it was asked casually. There was a certain amount of evidence that up to this point Helen Fayne had been sober and perfectly capable of driving her car. And she had left the party almost immediately afterwards. Thorne knew that the effects of liquor can be felt suddenly and unexpectedly, but if she had not had that last drink . . .

'Did I spill the whisky? A few drops, not more. It was the canapés that did the damage.' Merle was rueful.

'Then Miss Fayne drank the whisky you'd brought her?'

'Yes, Yes, she did, I'm sure she did, though—Oh, I can't really remember exactly what happened. But what does it matter, Superintendent? It's dreadful to suggest she was drunk. She wasn't. Why should her character be impugned like this? It's not right. The poor woman's dead, and she hurt no one in her manner of dying. Let her rest in peace.'

'I wonder if she is resting in peace,' Abbot said thoughtfully as he drove out of Windfield village and headed back towards Kidlington. 'At least we've tracked down the sex scandal, sir, though for the life of me I can't see what it's got to do with persuading Susan Hill to sell her share of South Winds.'

'*A* sex scandal, Sergeant,' Thorne corrected him. 'Probably one of many in the neighbourhood, if we but knew. I don't think Merle was really much help. He explained some of the anomalies in Muriel Fayne's death, but that's about all, though I suppose we'll have to get on to records about his so-called friend's death. As for Helen, I can't conceive of him trying to harm her. He wouldn't even admit she was a bit tight when she left the Clutton-Greys', though I got the impression that he thought she was.'

'So did I, sir,' Abbot agreed.

Thorne grew silent. Over what was left of the weekend he would have to write a report to be on the Chief Constable's desk on Monday morning, and so far he could see no reason why it should not be negative. He couldn't in good conscience recommend that more time and effort should be expended on this case. By now he had interviewed the possible suspects, those who might have something to gain from Helen Fayne's death. He had stirred up some muddy waters. He had caused a certain amount of gossip. But he had discovered nothing to support the theory that Helen had died other than accidentally, as a result of her own error or misjudgement, whatever the cause.

As for the incidents that had preceded her death, after the fall downstairs and the near-miss from the Esquimo sculpture, which could be put down to carelessness and accident respectively, Helen Fayne might have developed a mild paranoia, some form of persecution mania. There was little to support her claim about the bolting horse, or about the cause of Jeremy's illness. And her last and fatal accident could easily have been due to excess alcohol; whatever family and friends might say, she *had* been drinking, as everyone admitted and the PM had shown. And the effects of alcohol were variable and unpredictable.

True, more inquiries might produce other pointers, but they would mean more man-hours, probably spent without tangible result. Regretfully Superintendent Thorne made up his mind. He would recommend that the case be shelved.

Thorne was sure that this was the only possible decision in the circumstances, but what worried him was how to break it to the Bands. So the last message he needed when he reached his office at Headquarters was that Dr Band had telephoned, and would be grateful if the Superintendent would call him back as soon as possible at home. Thorne glanced at his overflowing in-tray, wished that he too were at home, and tapped out the number.

Mary Band answered the phone, 'I'll get him, George. He's mowing the lawn.'

At this news Detective-Superintendent George Thorne permitted himself a gleeful smile. He had no love of gardening—luckily Miranda enjoyed it—but he was expected to mow the grass, a task he hated, but undertook as a duty.

No longer envying the doctor, he greeted him with unusual cheerfulness.

Dick Band was not responsive to his banter. 'George, it concerns those tablets of Helen Fayne's—the ones Jeremy ate before he was taken ill. Assuming that hypnotics or narcotics—sleeping pills—were substituted for the antacids, I know where they could have come from.'

'Where?'

'As you know, Muriel Fayne suffered badly from arthritis. It gave her a lot of pain and kept her awake at night. I prescribed sleeping pills, but she always complained they weren't strong enough. And anyway, they were in capsule form, red and grey. But I suddenly remembered something. A few weeks before her death she went up to London to see a rheumatologist, and I looked up the letter he wrote me reporting on the consultation. He gave her some stronger sleeping pills, with strict instructions that she was only to take two a night, and never with liquor. These pills are not made up as capsules. They're white and circular and, except for faint markings, could easily be mistaken for antacid tablets.'

'You're suggesting Jeremy ate a couple of these?'

'Yes. With his small body weight that would have been enough to make him comatose. They'd probably have killed him if people hadn't acted quickly.'

'But what about his symptoms of food poisoning?'

'George, that's where I blame myself. I was careless. When Helen called, I was tired. I'd just come in from a difficult case. A patient of mine had died. And by the time I got to South Winds Jeremy was clearly recovering. Mrs Ferguson did say he'd been lethargic and sleepy, but I'm afraid I didn't pay much attention. He'd vomited. He'd had a loose motion. The women all said "food poisoning" and I accepted it. It was as simple as that.'

'And now you think it could have been old Mrs Fayne's sleeping pills?'

'Yes, I do. At least, I think there's support for Helen's story. A few of these strong drugs on top of her nightly whisky might well have been lethal.'

'Possibly, but—none of this *proves* anything, Dick. All we know is that some months ago there were strong sleeping pills similar in appearance to Helen's antacids in the Faynes' house. Helen never mentioned them, did she, when you were talking about her—her accidents?'

'No—no, she didn't.' Dick Band had begun to sound despondent. 'George, you don't seem very enthusiastic. Are you getting anywhere?'

'Not yet, but cheer up,' said Thorne, 'you never can tell.' He hadn't the heart to add that as far as he was concerned the inquiry had come to an end.

CHAPTER 16

'I've only had time to glance through your report quickly, Superintendent,' the Chief Constable said to George Thorne. 'Clearly there are one or two lines you haven't covered. For instance, the child Jeremy's not been questioned officially about the missing dart, or about these sleeping tablets he may have taken by mistake. But I appreciate that you and Sergeant Abbot have done a great deal in a short time, and I agree with your conclusion. Enough is enough. Unfortunately, limited manpower doesn't always permit us to do all we'd like, or perhaps should. So, albeit with some regret, I think we shall have to forget Miss Helen Fayne, unless anything new emerges.'

'Yes, sir.' Superintendent Thorne nodded; he couldn't help feeling in his bones that the decision was a pity, but it was what he had recommended and expected.

'Now,' said the Chief Constable, 'what else is there? First, this arson case in Banbury—'

Thorne turned his mind to other subjects. It was Monday morning, and the villains seemed to have been busy over the weekend. With these files added to its present commitments it looked as if there was going to be plenty to occupy the Serious Crime Squad in the coming week.

A tap on the door and the entrance of Philip Midvale's secretary interrupted their discussion. 'Sir, I'm sorry, but there's an urgent phone call for the Superintendent from Dr Band.'

'Right. Put it through here.' The Chief Constable gestured to Thorne to use his phone.

'Thank you, sir.' The Superintendent picked up the receiver, waited until the connection was made and said, 'Thorne here.' He listened. 'What? When? Another *accident*? Dear God! Yes, of course I'll be along as soon as possible. But where is he now?' He listened. 'Anything else I should know?' He listened again, then let the receiver fall back on its rest and sat, staring straight ahead, apparently unaware of the Chief Constable across the desk.

Midvale, who had opened a file when Thorne began to speak, had got no further than the first sentence. He looked up, startled by the dismay in the Superintendent's voice: George Thorne, he knew, was not given to displays of emotion. When Thorne remained motionless, he said sharply, 'What is it, man? Is it your wife?'

'No. No, sir.' Thorne heaved a sigh. 'I'm responsible for something dreadful,' he said.

Midvale waited patiently. Thorne sat, head lowered, for what seemed like a long minute, pulling at his moustache, and obviously thinking hard. At last he raised his eyes and met the Chief Constable's anxious gaze.

'I let everyone concerned believe it was the vicar, Timothy Merle, who had urged these inquiries into Helen Fayne's death. And now, sir, someone's tried to kill *him*. Indeed, they may have succeeded.'

'What happened?'

'No one knows. He's unconscious in hospital in Oxford with multiple injuries. But apparently he was found early this morning by David Castle—you remember, sir, the owner of the Derwent Stables—when he was exercising some horses. Merle was lying in a hedge with his bicycle— or what remained of it—on top of him. Seemingly it was a hit-and-run job, and that's how it's being treated at the moment by the Colombury police.'

'Another accident? Another coincidence?'

'Quite, sir. It's hard to believe in the circumstances, isn't it?'

'Almost impossible, I'd say, Superintendent.'

'Incidentally, Band says Merle was found in the lane where Helen Fayne's horse bolted, if that's worth anything.' Thorne shook his head. 'Sir, this need not have happened. Sergeant Abbot warned me, but I paid no attention. It's my fault. I take full responsibility. I wanted to stir things up so that someone would make a mistake, and now this poor wretched man's paying the price. According to Band, his chances of survival are only moderate.'

Philip Midvale was a thoughtful man, but his practical common sense was one of the qualities that made him a good Chief Constable. He could understand that Superintendent Thorne, for once in his life, had been badly shaken by the result of his own actions, and blamed himself for lacking the imagination to foresee what might happen. He realized, too, that the last thing Thorne wanted was sympathy.

He said, 'Superintendent, you've stirred things up, which is what you intended. Someone *has* made a mistake, which was also your intention. Now it's for you to take advantage of it.'

'Yes, sir. Thank you, sir—very much.'

Superintendent George Thorne was already on his feet, his face expressionless. He made for the door immediately. The Chief Constable let him go, knowing full well that the case of Helen Fayne was not yet closed.

Thorne spent several minutes giving Sergeant Abbot instructions, then drove himself into Oxford. At the hospital he parked in a space marked 'Doctors Only' and, stalking to the front of the small but tidy queue at the Inquiries desk, produced his warrant card and demanded to see the doctor in charge of the Reverend Timothy Merle. The receptionist picked up her phone at once. No one in the queue objected. In minutes a nurse appeared, and he was ushered into a doctor's office.

Thorne came to the point at once. 'It's extremely important that I talk to Mr Merle as soon as possible,' he said, without greeting or preamble.

The doctor was young, but not to be bullied. 'A matter of life and death, Superintendent? There is a uniformed man with him all the time, you know.'

'It's not life and death, Doctor. It's a matter of death and death. And we don't want any more, do we? How is Merle?'

The doctor was taken aback by Thorne's brusque manner, but he reminded himself that he wasn't dealing with a relative, and had no need to mince words. He said, 'I wouldn't like to bet on his survival. The odds are against him, but he might make it. As for talking to him, you can try. I doubt if it'll do him any harm. But I warn you: he drifts in and out of consciousness and what he says doesn't make sense.'

'I'll risk it. It may to me.'

'Right. I'll take you to him, then. Needless to say, he's in the ICU.'

Thorne followed the doctor to a lift which they had to share with two orderlies and an unconscious body on a stretcher, along a corridor smelling of antiseptic, past hurrying nurses and two doctors having an earnest conversation, while a loudspeaker demanded the immediate presence of Mr Brown in Ward Two. The impression was one of bustle and suppressed urgency. By contrast the intensive care unit was a haven of peace, with no sound except for quiet footsteps, the soft bleep of monitors and the murmur of machinery.

One nurse sat in front of a bank of television screens, watching over the patients who were segregated in cubicles. Two others moved around the unit. None of them paid much attention when the doctor introduced Superintendent Thorne, and none showed any interest in the fact that he was a police officer.

'Mr Merle's in Number Six,' she said. 'At the end. There's a policeman with him.'

'Thank you,' Thorne said, and was surprised how loud his voice sounded.

With a brief nod of farewell the doctor left them, and as quietly as he could Thorne went along to the far cubicle, where the Reverend Timothy Merle lay in his high hospital bed, so still that for a moment Thorne thought he was dead. But suddenly his lips parted and he murmured something.

The uniformed man stood up when the Superintendent identified himself, but shook his head in response to Thorne's whispered question, 'Anything?'

'Nothing useful, sir.'

Thorne dismissed the man temporarily and took his place in the chair beside the bed, careful not to disarrange any of the tubes attached to Merle's body. He looked at his watch, wondering how long he could afford to stay there, waiting, waiting, perhaps in vain, for the parson to have a period of lucidity. Time passed. Thorne tried not to fidget. Merle's face, as white as the bandage round his head, began to seem like a reproach to the Superintendent.

Then, without warning, Timothy Merle opened his eyes, and they were bright with intelligence. Thorne leant towards him, to bring himself into Merle's field of view. For half a minute the two men regarded each other, before Merle managed to smile sleepily.

Thorne said, 'Mr Merle. I'm sorry you've been hurt. Do you know how it happened?'

'Telephone call,' Merle said.

His voice was faint, scarcely more than a whisper, and Thorne thought he might have misheard. He leant closer still. Merle closed his eyes and Thorne was afraid he was about to slide into unconsciousness again. But it seemed he was trying to rally his strength.

'Phone call,' he said, distinctly this time. 'Urgent. I went. Quickest way. Down the lane. On my bike. Bright light— blinded me. And roaring noise. Like God.'

'What time?' asked Thorne, and realized that he was copying the parson's staccato shorthand. 'What time did you get the phone call and leave your house?' he repeated.

'Ten? Eleven? I'd—dropped off—in chair.'

It was better than nothing, but the Superintendent had hoped for an exact time. 'Did you have the television on, Mr Merle?'

'Don't have TV. Too expensive. Radio on Three. Music.'

The parson might have been rambling, but for the moment there seemed nothing wrong with his process of reasoning, Thorne thought. Merle had grasped the point about television instantly. It was a pity he couldn't have named a programme. Radio Three broadcast music most of the day, and was little help in fixing the time.

A nurse appeared at the entrance to the cubicle. 'I'm afraid that's enough for now. The patient's vital signs show he's getting a little excited.'

Thorne stood up immediately, but to his surprise Merle reached out a hand to prevent his departure. Thorne looked at the nurse, who hesitated but said, 'Two more minutes, then,' and left them.

'About Helen. Was thinking. Lied to you,' Merle said. 'Wrong, but—'

He seemed unable to continue, and Thorne tried to prompt him. 'Helen Fayne. Yes, I think I understand. You lied—about her being drunk when she drove away from the Clutton-Greys'?' It was a guess. The Superintendent was far from sure that he did understand. But Merle nodded fractionally in agreement. 'It was because you didn't want her good name to suffer?' Thorne added.

'Yes. Besides—must have been last drink I—I brought her. Not drunk before.' Timothy Merle was making a huge effort. 'Behind her—on drive. Bounced on car seat. No— no belt. Arms flapped. Bird. Broken wing.' Merle's eyelids dropped, his mouth opened, he gave a low moan and was still.

Thorne was on his feet as a buzzer sounded, but two of the nurses were already there, one pulling the cardiac arrest trolley, the other stripping back the bedclothes from Merle's body. The third nurse continued to watch the monitoring equipment, but spoke urgently into a phone. She gestured to the door when she saw Thorne, and the Superintendent obediently left the room.

Above the door of the intensive care unit a red light was flashing. The doctor whom Thorne had met earlier came dashing down the corridor, followed by two other men. To avoid them the Superintendent stood back against the wall beside the constable waiting outside. Thorne had never felt so useless and unwanted in his life.

He spoke briefly to the uniformed officer, then went down in the lift, out of the hospital and sat in his car. He pushed to the back of his mind thoughts of what might be happening to Timothy Merle, and forced himself to concentrate on what the parson had said about Helen Fayne, relating it to the other accounts of her behaviour at the Clutton-Greys' party.

Helen Fayne, it was agreed, had had two, or possibly three, whiskies diluted with soda. They had not been especially strong drinks, and she was used to liquor. She had shown no signs of being affected by them until she was about to leave—after the minor disaster with the plate of canapés, after she had drunk that last drink. Then, completely out of character, she had driven in an abandoned fashion down the drive and into a stone wall.

She had driven, Merle had said—and Thorne realized that he believed the vicar's evidence—as if she were some kind of bird. Detective-Superintendent Thorne wouldn't have claimed to be an expert on drugs, but over the years he had acquired a fair knowledge of the subject, and at once he thought of LSD or something of that kind.

It fitted, he realized. These drugs were fast-acting. They produced illusions. One could have been added to Helen's drink, which might well have been put down somewhere during the commotion over the spilt food. No one remembered after all this time exactly who had been where, and it wouldn't have been a difficult act to conceal.

And later, handed the glass, Helen would have drunk its contents automatically, not noticing any odd taste in her natural agitation. If she had failed to drink it, the glass would have been washed up anyway, so there would have been no evidence left behind.

The killer, Thorne thought, was purposeful and determined, a cat playing with a mouse, but a cat with the firm intention of eventually eating the mouse. He mentally reviewed the possible suspects; he found it hard to see any of them as a cold-blooded murderer. Yet one of them, he was sure, had planned Helen Fayne's death and, fearing that Timothy Merle might innocently know too much, had tried to destroy him too.

Superintendent Thorne turned his ignition on, and then turned it off again. He realized that, much as he hated the prospect, he couldn't possibly leave the hospital without discovering whether his ploy had killed Merle or not. He was lucky. He was about to face the Inquiries desk again, when the doctor came into the entrance hall.

'There you are, Superintendent,' he said. 'I've been looking all over for you.'

'How is he?' Thorne asked at once.

'He survived that crisis, and his condition's stable. He's no worse. That's about all I can say now. Phone later if you don't want to wait.'

'Do you think my questioning—?'

'Brought it on? Who can tell? Anyway, I hope it was worth while.'

'It was, Doctor. It was. The constable's back with him, I hope?'

'Oh yes.'

'Thank you, Doctor. Thank you.'

When he reached Headquarters Thorne went straight to his office, where he found Sergeant Abbot sitting behind his desk. Abbot got up hurriedly.

'Sorry, sir, but I seem to have been on the phone all the morning, and it was easier taking the calls here.'

'That's all right. Any news?' Thorne reclaimed his seat.

'Not about the Reverend Merle's accident, sir. It's a bit soon for that. But, as you instructed, I've made sure the incident's being treated as a possible case of attempted murder. The scene of crime boys should be there by now.'

'Fine. Between you and me, Sergeant, I'm absolutely certain he was run down deliberately. However, I'll explain later. Go on.'

'Mrs Bridget Drayton phoned. She said she'd heard from her daughter that we'd been making inquiries about a dart. When she was sorting out her sister's things, she'd found one wrapped in a handkerchief at the back of a drawer in Miss Helen Fayne's bedroom. She'd thought it a bit odd, but not of any particular significance, and she added it to the pile Mrs Ferguson was to throw away. So it's gone, sir. The dustmen collected the next day.'

'Damn! Still, we could hardly have asked for a search warrant, could we? I wonder what else she threw out, not that we can blame her.'

'All the contents of the medicine cupboard, it seems. I asked her what was in it, sir. She seemed surprised, but said not much. Apart from her antacid tablets, Miss Fayne didn't believe in "pills and potions"; those were her words. But what there was Mrs Ferguson put down the toilet.'

Superintendent Thorne sighed heavily. 'Any *good* news, Sergeant?'

'I don't know how good it is, sir, but the Drugs Squad say that about a year ago Peter Drayton was caught in possession of a little cannabis resin, and got off with a caution. Not too serious these days, one could argue. Off the record they said he was pretty lucky, because he's got some dubious friends. It could mean nothing, but—'

'M—mm. Buts and ifs. Yes,' Thorne said, and thought of the Reverend Timothy Merle. 'An early lunch,' he added suddenly and decisively. 'Then off to Colombury, Sergeant, and the village of Windfield.'

CHAPTER 17

After an early lunch—Superintendent Thorne in his mess, and Sergeant Abbot in the canteen; even in today's demo-cratized police force the distinction still existed—the two police officers once again set off for Colombury. Before leaving Kidlington Thorne phoned the hospital and made another inquiry after the Reverend Timothy Merle. All he got was a routine answer, 'No change; stable and comfortable.'

'Probably means he's stuffed full of drugs and isn't being any trouble,' commented Abbot, who had a cynical distrust of doctors and hospitals.

'At least it means he's still alive,' Thorne said thankfully.

'And that's something surprising. I gathered from Sergeant Court, sir.' Abbot grinned. 'He called it a "blooming miracle".'

Sergeant Court repeated this assertion when they arrived at the police station in Colombury. He had been in a state of barely-suppressed excitement since receiving the news of a possible murder on his patch. 'They're finding bits of the vicar's bike strewn about for yards, sir. Mind you, it was an old rattler of a bike, but all the same it must have been hit pretty hard to make it fly around like that.'

'Let's hope the bits'll give us some help as to what hit it,' Thorne said soberly.

'You'll be going along to the scene now, sir?' Court asked. 'Do you want me—'

'No. No need, Sergeant. We know the way, and I'm sure you've plenty to occupy you.'

A little reluctantly Court said, 'That I have sir. There's this break-in last night at the Drayton Galleries and—'

'What?'

'The Galleries? Well, it seems someone phoned the Draytons to say a man had been seen on the roof of the Galleries, trying to get in through a skylight, and Mr Drayton had better come down. So, of course, he leapt in his car and came as quick as he could.'

'But when he got there he found no sign that anyone had been trying to effect an entrance?'

Sergeant Court stared at the Superintendent in some surprise. 'How—how did you know that, sir?'

Thorne didn't answer directly. Instead, he said thoughtfully, 'Drayton didn't phone the police before he left home? It would have been the obvious thing to do. You'd have got there a lot sooner than he could. For that matter, why didn't the original informant call you?'

Court thought this over for a moment and then said, 'I don't know about the original informant, but Mrs Drayton phoned us, to say her husband was on the way. She sounded a bit worried, sir, and I went at once. I didn't have to dress or anything.'

The Superintendent grunted. 'So this was fairly early, was it? What time?'

'Half past ten, sir, or soon after. Channel Three news had just finished,' said Sergeant Court promptly. 'I had a good look round before Mr Drayton arrived, but there was nothing suspicious, as you guessed, sir.'

Thorne grunted again, and then said abruptly that he and Abbot must be off to the scene of the vicar's accident. Court, who had given up being surprised by the Superintendent's reactions, saw them to the door of the station.

'Pity Peter Drayton wasn't at home at the time. He could have gone with his father. Then Mrs Drayton needn't have worried,' Court remarked as they were on the point of leaving.

Thorne stopped. 'Where *was* Peter Drayton? Do you know, Sergeant?'

'Yes, I do, sir. He'd been visiting a friend in Oxford, he said. Funny thing, he saw the lights on in the Galleries, and turned up just as we were all leaving. A bit late in the day, like.'

'Funny thing, indeed!' Thorne said to Abbot as they turned into the High Street. 'I'd like to know more about this phone call and the supposed break-in. Two false alarms at approximately the same time are too much of a coincidence in my book. However, let's go and have a look at the scene of the real crime, Sergeant.'

The lane where Vain Glory, pierced by a dart, had bolted with Helen Fayne, the lane where there seemed every likelihood that someone had driven at Timothy Merle with intent to kill, was barricaded at either end. Shoulder to shoulder, uniformed officers crept slowly over the ground, examining every inch. Any find of interest was put at once into a plastic bag and labelled. It was an impressive display of team work.

Superintendent Thorne regarded it with approval. 'Any joy?' he asked the inspector in charge of the operation, when he came forward to greet the visitors.

'Not much, sir,' the inspector reported. 'We've found the spot where the collision took place. There are no sudden brake marks, no signs of a skid. The vehicle didn't mount the grass verge. All the signs are it drove straight at the unfortunate clergyman, hit him hard and continued on. The bicycle was demolished, but Mr Merle was almost certainly thrown up in the air and over the bonnet. I'll show you where he landed—in the hedge. It was the hedge that saved his life—if he's still alive.'

'Just—but only just,' Thorne said grimly.

'Mind you, sir, a good defence lawyer would say it was a dark night, the bike wasn't properly lit, and the driver

thought the bump was a stone or a branch of a tree so didn't
stop.'

'Let's start worrying about that when we've caught
him, Inspector.' Thorne didn't mention the prospect of
other charges. 'First, we need to try to identify the
vehicle. Shouldn't the force of the impact have left traces on
it?

'I'm not so sure, sir. Come and look at this.'

The Inspector led Thorne and Abbot a few yards further
down the lane. Lying on the grass verge was a large clear
plastic bag. Inside they could see what appeared to be a roll
of thick brown corrugated cardboard.

'We found it in the field, sir. It looks as if it was chucked
over the hedge. It could be irrelevant, but my guess is it
was tied over the front of the vehicle—you know, the way
some people tie cardboard over their radiators in very cold
weather. And I think there are some bloodstains on it.
Forensic will tell us, of course. But if I'm right, and it
was meant as a form of protection, there may be precious
few marks on the vehicle. After all, a man on a bicycle's not
a very heavy object to crash into.' He paused for a moment,
then added tentatively, 'But it's relevant to premeditation,
isn't it, sir?'

'Indeed,' said Thorne shortly.

'But why discard it, sir?' Abbot asked Thorne as they
drove slowly up the Clutton-Greys' drive to the Hall. 'If it
hadn't been thrown away there, we wouldn't have known
it existed.'

'True, Sergeant,' the Superintendent agreed. 'On the
other hand, what on earth are you going to do with it? If
you take it in your car, it might leave traces—blood, say—
and that's the very thing you want to avoid. No, the best
bet was to discard it, and hope it wouldn't be found until
there had been a good downpour of rain and it had more or
less disintegrated.'

Abbot had been thinking. 'But what about *before* the crime, sir?'

'Exactly, Sergeant. It was dark, of course. There wouldn't be many people around at the time, and the car's own headlights would dazzle a chance observer, so there was every possibility the cardboard wouldn't be noticed. Still, it would have been a risk to drive it far with the cardboard in place. It points to someone living pretty close to the lane, wouldn't you say, Sergeant?'

Sergeant Abbot nodded. 'The Clutton-Greys are the closest of the people involved,' he remarked tentatively.

'Ye—es,' Thorne said without any great conviction as Abbot drew up in front of the Hall. He undid his seat-belt, but sat, ruminating—not about the corrugated board, but about Paul Drayton and the phone call concerning the intruder at the Galleries that Drayton claimed to have received. The story continued to worry the Superintendent.

After a long wait in the hall a manservant showed the two police officers into what he called the morning-room—a bright, sunny room at the rear of the house. It seemed as if the Clutton-Grey family had been assembled—almost posed—there to meet the authorities. Sir Reginald stood with his back to a hearth in which glowed the imitation coals of a modern gas fire. His mother, the dowager, sat upright in a high-backed chair, and Sir Reginald's wife, dressed for riding even to a hard hat, was gazing impatiently out of the window.

Clutton-Grey wasted no time with greetings. He attacked at once. 'Superintendent,' he said angrily, 'this is beyond a joke. For the last few days you and your Sergeant have been all over the village and round about, asking the most extraordinary questions. As far as I can make out, the suggestion seems to be that Miss Helen Fayne was—was poisoned or something at that party my wife and I gave.

And now because poor Timothy Merle was knocked off that stupid bicycle of his in the lane just beyond our grounds, we're surrounded with the police. People are beginning to look at me and—and turn away. Really, Superintendent, it's not good enough.'

Thorne let him finish, a little weakly the Superintendent thought. The dowager, apparently agreeing with Thorne, was regarding her son with clear contempt. Kathleen Clutton-Grey had started to beat her riding-crop against a boot; she was making it clear that, whatever the trouble was, it had nothing to do with her. None of them would have been flattered by Thorne's thoughts.

'I'm sorry if you're being inconvenienced, sir,' Thorne said, 'but you can't hold the police responsible for local gossip. Anyway, the best means of putting an end to rumour, as I'm sure you'll agree, is to establish the truth, so I've no doubt we can count on your help.'

There was silence, except for a warning cough from Sergeant Abbot, which Thorne ignored. He had decided that the weapon most likely to shake anything out of the Clutton-Greys was bluntness. If Sir Reginald wanted to use his influence and complain to the Chief Constable later, he could damn well do his worst.

He pressed ahead. 'To start with, perhaps you'd all be good enough to tell me where you were between ten and midnight last evening.'

To his surprise it was old Lady-Clutton-Grey who answered first, though after a disapproving pause. 'I was in bed, Superintendent Thorne. My son came to say good night to me, and we watched the ten o'clock news together on the small television set I have in my room. My room, incidentally, is on the far side of the house from the lane, so we saw nothing and heard nothing of Mr Merle's accident.' She turned her head, and smiled at her daughter-in-law, inviting her to answer Thorne's question for herself, but the smile was without warmth, the Superintendent noticed.

'If you're asking me, I was out,' Kathleen Clutton-Grey said at length. 'Playing bridge at the Wilkinsons'. Mrs Slinter made up the fourth. You can check with them if you like. Jean Slinter had a headache so we broke up early. I was home soon after eleven. I didn't come down the lane, and I never saw the Hon. Tim.'

'The Hon. Tim?' Thorne queried.

'The Honourable Timothy Merle,' she explained. 'Didn't you know, Superintendent? He's the youngest son of an Irish peer. Completely impoverished, of course. His brother got whatever there was to inherit, and turned it into a tidy fortune, but I'm afraid the Hon. Tim's been something of a failure.'

'He's certainly quite inadequate as a vicar.' It was the elder Lady Clutton-Grey who spoke, but it was obvious that for once the two women were in accord. She added, 'And now, Superintendent, if there's nothing else, we're all busy people, even me. I have letters to write.'

Abbot saw the Superintendent's mouth grow thin at this casual dismissal, not so much of the police as of the Reverend Timothy Merle. Hurriedly, fearing an acid comment from Thorne that might give the Clutton-Greys a valid cause for complaint, the Sergeant had a violent burst of coughing. Thorne gave him a glance of mock sympathy, and waited until the noise ended.

Then, turning to Kathleen Clutton-Grey, he said, 'There is one thing, Lady Clutton-Grey. Would you be good enough to tell me about this scandal that's connected with the Faynes and the Draytons. And please don't say you've no idea what I'm talking about, because I can always ask Mrs Slinter.'

Kathleen Clutton-Grey hesitated. Then she said, 'Evidently you're not above listening to other people's private conversations, Superintendent. Or, to give what you were

doing its right name, eavesdropping. It's rather an unpleasant word, isn't it, Superintendent?'

'So is blackmail, Lady Clutton-Grey.'

There was a sudden, heavy silence. The only member
of the party who seemed unconcerned was Superintendent Thorne. He continued to look steadily and inquiringly at Kathleen Clutton-Grey, who had flushed with
anger.

'Now see here, Superintendent! What is this? You can't
come into this house and make unpleasant insinuations, you
know.' Sir Reginald at last found his voice. 'I won't have it.
I have a position in this community and—'

'Be quiet, Reggie,' his mother commanded. 'Kathleen is
quite capable of speaking for herself.'

Indeed, by now she was. Sir Reginald's intervention had
given her a moment to think, and she was as quick-witted
as she was attractive. She had realized that her best course
was to cooperate with Thorne.

She gave a little laugh. 'I'm afraid you overheard only
part of the conversation, Superintendent. However, no
matter. The scandal we were talking about is that some
years ago the much respected Helen Fayne had an *affaire*.
She became pregnant and underwent an abortion. It wasn't
illegal, though it was done privately. After all, she was much
too old to have a first child, and the mental stress would
have been dreadful. Mind you, the story may not be true. I
haven't checked. Why should I? You'll have to ask Mrs
Slinter.'

She was mocking him, Thorne knew, but he didn't care.
He was busy digesting this unexpected piece of information,
unexpected because he couldn't picture Helen Fayne in this
new role. 'Was this before Miss Fayne returned to Windfield
to look after her mother?' he asked.

Kathleen Clutton-Grey shrugged. 'I believe not,' she said.
'But really I don't know. Nor can I tell you who the father

was, Superintendent.' She laughed. 'All I can suggest is that you ask Jean Slinter. She may know.'

'What a bitch!' Sergeant Abbot said in disgust as they drove away from the Hall. 'Do you think she'll be on the blower now, warning the Slinter woman, sir?'

'I rather doubt it,' said Thorne.

Certainly Jean Slinter seemed surprised to see them. The Slinters' house, though not as imposing as the Hall, was big, modern, split-level and clearly expensive. Mrs Slinter opened the front door to them herself, and took them into a room she called the library, though it was dominated by a snooker table and held few books.

'Well, what is it?' she said without bothering to invite them to sit down.

Thorne asked about the bridge party the previous evening, and she confirmed Kathleen Clutton-Grey's story. Then he turned to Helen Fayne's abortion, and it was at once apparent that she'd had no warning of his knowledge of or interest in this.

'Well really, Superintendent!' she said. 'One tells a friend something in strict confidence, and the next moment it's become the subject of a police inquiry. I simply don't understand it.'

'Mrs Slinter, we need this information, and we shall get it in the end. You could save us a lot of time and trouble.'

'Yes,' she said thoughtfully, after a pause. 'Yes.' Like Kathleen Clutton-Grey, she was realizing that cooperation was the best policy. Eventually she sat down and waved Thorne and Abbot to chairs. 'It was twelve years ago,' she began.

'Are you sure of the date?' Thorne asked. It was well after Helen Fayne had arrived back in Windfield.

'Quite sure. It was the year I married Frank, and I didn't work after that. But at the time I was a nurse . . .'

She produced the address of the private nursing home in London, and the name of the doctor who had performed the abortion. She stressed the fact that there had been nothing illegal about it, but some of the patients were unmarried, or had husbands who had been abroad at the relevant time. The utmost discretion had been demanded of all the staff.

'Of course the place kept records, but the staff knew some of the patients only by their room numbers. For instance, I called Helen Fayne "Madam", and she called me "Nurse". She wasn't there long, as there were no complications. A couple of days and she was gone. She had no reason to remember me, but I remembered her. She was an odd-looking woman, not attractive, older than most of the patients and very sharp-tongued.'

'When you came across her here in Windfield, did you ever remind her where you'd met before, Mrs Slinter?'

'No. Of course not. And apart from Lady Clutton-Grey I never told anyone.'

'I see. Now, what about the father? Have you any idea?'

'None at all. As far as I'm concerned, it could have been anyone on earth. I just don't know.'

They learnt no more from Jean Slinter. Nor were the Hills, whom they tried next, of any help. Susan said she had gone to bed early the previous night; Andrew said he had been driving back from Coriston, and couldn't say when he got home, but his wife had been asleep. And Gavin Drayton. when they reached Oxford and questioned him, maintained that he had been in his flat all the evening, alone.

'We're going to be busy tomorrow, Abbot,' Thorne predicted. 'Let's try and get an early start.'

CHAPTER 18

The last place in the world Superintendent George Thorne wanted to be was sitting at his desk. He had hoped to go to London to check personally on Jean Slinter's story of Helen Fayne's abortion. However, the Chief Constable, who was less impressed than Thorne by the importance of the new information, had pointed out with some asperity that such instruments as telephones and Telex existed, and that the Met could do the work more quickly, possibly more efficiently, and—from the point of view of the Thames Valley Police—more cheaply. Thorne had found no immediate answer to this pointed comment.

So he sat at his desk, quite aware that the Chief Constable had reason on his side, but still seething inwardly. When he knew—or thought he knew—that cases were beginning to reach their climactic moments, he hated to be inactive. He had dealt with the Met, explained what was needed, and now had merely to wait for their reply. Not, he thought dourly, that there was much doubt about it. The Slinter woman couldn't have invented her extraordinary story. The trouble was that the Chief Constable was probably right, and the story itself, even if proved to be true, quite irrelevant; twelve years was a very long time to harbour a motive for murder in silence. Or had the father perhaps just discovered what had happened to his child? It was possible, Thorne supposed.

The father? All the evidence suggested that the killer was someone close to the family, or living close by and aware of the family's routines; on the assumption that the killer and the father were one and the same, the father must be close to the family, too. Paul Drayton? His sons? But Peter and

Gavin would have been only in their late teens twelve years ago. Reginald Clutton-Grey, who had certainly not been faithful to one wife? Frank Slinter? That would have been an odd coincidence, but coincidences did happen, and he had apparently chosen to come and live near the Faynes, whatever the significance of that. Then there was Henry Wilkinson—a long shot, certainly, who hadn't yet been interviewed—but an *affaire* with her husband might account for Helen Fayne's obvious dislike of Mrs Wilkinson. David Castle; also a very long shot. Perhaps Mrs Ferguson had a husband . . .

Thorne pulled himself together and shook his head as his imagination wandered so far afield. He realized he had forgotten Andrew Hill. But Hill wasn't thirty yet and, like the Drayton boys, would have been very young for Helen, but differences in age, or class, or circumstances, sometimes didn't matter in affairs of the heart.

Again the Superintendent pulled himself up sharply; he was starting to think like a romantic novel. But there was a point here somewhere. Helen hadn't necessarily been looking for a great long-lasting love. Indeed, such a romance was unlikely in a small community like Windfield, for it could hardly have failed to become generally known—or at least rumoured. Perhaps, Thorne reflected, he should have called on that postmistress—what was her name? Then he thought: No, more probably Helen's lapse had been a one-off, and she had been careless and unlucky. Poor Helen Fayne; Thorne had almost grown fond of her in the course of the investigation.

His phone rang in time to prevent further pointless rumination. It was Merle's doctor, to whom the Superintendent had previously put in a call. The parson had had a good night, and was reasonably comfortable. X-rays showed a hairline fracture of the skull, but the periods of unconsciousness were growing shorter. He couldn't yet be said to be out of danger, but there were reasonable grounds for optimism. Merle had asked that his bishop be informed, but not his family.

'Could I come and talk to him again this afternoon?' Thorne asked.

'Why not? But take care. We don't want another cardiac crisis.'

'I'll do my best,' Thorne promised.

In view of Timothy Merle's past history, Thorne had hesitated to include him in his mental list of possible fathers, and this opinion was reinforced now that the vicar himself had suffered an attack. But Merle and Helen Fayne had undoubtedly been close friends; Merle had admitted they had a lot in common. And he was her—what was the right expression?—her clergyman? Her confessor—perhaps that was the word. It was possible that Helen had confided in him. Come to that, another possible confidante was Mary Band.

Thorne reached out for the phone. Then he withdrew his hand. He really must get down to work. He had wasted enough time already, considering what was probably a totally false trail. Reluctantly he started on the file on top of the pile in his in-tray.

Coincidentally, it was the official report of Merle's so-called accident. Largely technical, it told the Superintendent little that he had not already known or surmised. There were no indications that the driver of the vehicle had tried to avoid the cyclist, or made any effort to help his victim after the collision. So far no one had been traced who had seen a car with corrugated cardboard tied over its front end, but the piece found in the field had definitely been in contact with Merle's cycle.

Thorne put it aside, and doggedly started on the remainder of the files awaiting his attention, mostly concerned with other cases. Officers came and went at intervals, with information or queries. Only once was an interruption welcome—Sergeant Abbot, with the Superintendent's mid-morning coffee and biscuits. The telephone rang far too often. And, shortly before lunch, a Telex from the Met confirmed Mrs Slinter's tale of Helen Fayne's abortion.

George Thorne drew a deep breath, while he hesitated for a moment. Then almost viciously he punched out Abbot's extension. 'Here, Sergeant,' he said shortly, 'as soon as you can.'

Abbot arrived within a couple of minutes, trying not to appear anxious. 'Sir?' he said.

'A car at once,' said Thorne. 'We're off to Colombury. We'll stop at the first good pub for a pint and a sandwich or two.'

'Yes, sir,' said Abbot enthusiastically. His morning, too, had been occupied with what he considered routine tasks.

The Superintendent smiled, pleased with his decisiveness, and stroked his moustache thoughtfully.

But, to Abbot's surprise, after his initial haste, the Superintendent made no attempt to hurry over lunch. He needed time, he said, to plan his campaign. In fact, it was not until shortly before three that the two officers arrived in Colombury. They parked their car, and went straight to the Drayton Galleries. There they found Paul and Biddy Drayton, with Peter. Clearly their visit was not welcome.

'What is it now, Superintendent?' Biddy demanded. 'If you've come about that dart I found in my sister's drawer I'm sorry I threw it away, but how could I know you'd be so interested in it?'

'Why *are* you interested in it?' Peter asked.

'Please!' said Thorne. 'Forget the dart. Mrs Drayton, Mr Drayton, might we have a word with you in private. Perhaps your son here could look after the shop for a few minutes.'

Resignedly Biddy led the way to the office at the rear of

the premises. It was such a small room that, with the desk and the rest of its contents, the four of them seemed to fill it. Paul Drayton perched on a corner of the desk, while his wife and the Superintendent occupied the only available chairs. Sergeant Abbot was forced to stand by the door, excellently placed to observe, and suggesting rather ominously that he wouldn't hesitate to stop anyone who tried to leave.

Thorne opened the proceedings, and Biddy reacted angrily. She vehemently denied that her sister had ever been pregnant, let alone had an abortion. She said the idea was ludicrous rubbish, and appealed to her husband for support. He agreed that it was utter nonsense. When Thorne insisted that proof was available, Biddy claimed that mistaken identity must be the answer. Eventually, however, both the Draytons grew silent.

'I'm sorry this has been such a shock to you,' Thorne said. 'I was hoping perhaps you could help us.'

'How?' asked Paul. 'Helen—Helen's dead. For God's sake, can't you leave it at that? Why should you care about something that happened—might have happened—years ago?'

'I'm sorry,' Thorne apologized again. 'I had no wish to upset you. I'm seeking information about a certain individual, and this might have been relevant.'

Neither of the Draytons produced the obvious question arising from this elliptic remark, and Thorne rose from his chair. Silently Paul Drayton saw the two officers to the door of the Galleries. As he opened it for them, Thorne remarked casually, 'I gather you had an attempted break-in here last night.'

'Someone was seen on the roof,' Drayton said curtly. 'He didn't get in. There was no one around when Sergeant Court arrived.'

'A hoax call, d'you think?'

'I don't know, but I doubt it. Why should anyone—'

'You didn't recognize the voice?'

'My wife took the call. She just said it was a man. He didn't give a name, and she'd certainly have mentioned it if she'd known who he was. I expect a passer-by saw, or thought he saw, someone, and decided to be a good Samaritan. Is it important?'

'Probably not,' Thorne said lightly.

The pavement was crowded with afternoon shoppers, mostly women and children, some with prams or pushchairs. It was impossible for Thorne and Abbot to hold a coherent conversation until they reached their car. Then Thorne asked the Sergeant for his impression of the Draytons.

'I'd say they knew about Helen, sir—both of them,' Abbot replied at once. 'They denied it too violently. What shocked them was that *we* should know. I was puzzled you didn't press them a little harder, sir,' he added tentatively. 'We might have got the father's name.'

Thorne shook his head. 'I don't think so, Sergeant. Even if they know it, which isn't certain. I don't believe either of them would have told us.' To Abbot's surprise he began to get out of the car again. 'Fruit,' he said, over his shoulder. 'Grapes, I suppose—for the Reverend the Honourable—or is it the Honourable the Reverend?—Timothy. I can't visit a nobleman empty-handed for a second time, Abbot.'

'No, sir. Indeed not,' Abbot said with a straight face.

Five minutes later Superintendent Thorne returned, carrying a small wicker basket containing a variety of fruits. It was covered in plastic, and had a large blue bow on the handle. When Abbot gaped at it, he said, 'I know it's a bit fancy, but at least it might amuse the man, if he's conscious when we get there.'

Timothy Merle was conscious, and able to appreciate Thorne's gift. 'I like the bow,' he said, and smiled weakly.

Merle was still in his cubicle in the ICU, and to the

Superintendent he looked dreadfully ill, though the prognosis was improving, the doctor claimed. Merle was doing much better than had been expected. With any luck he should be out of the wood in a day or two.

'Kind of you to come,' he said. 'Or isn't this a social call?'

'Not altogether, I regret to say,' Thorne admitted. 'There are a couple of points I hope you can help us with.' He shifted his chair closer to the bed, so that Merle would have to make only a minimal effort to hear him. 'The night you were knocked off your bike, you received a phone call. Who was it from?'

'The daughter of an old farmer, Charles Gotobed. Everyone in the district knows him and his family, and he's one of my small flock. He's been ill for some time, and when his daughter said he was dying and wanted me, naturally I went at once.'

'Did you recognize the voice?'

'Not—not particularly. I didn't think about it.'

'And these Gotobeds—the quickest way, the obvious way, for you to get to them from your vicarage was along the lane by the Clutton-Greys' estate?'

'Yes, but . . . Superintendent, you can't be suggesting—? These Gotobeds are good people.'

'I'm sure they are. And I'm also sure that when we check we'll find they never phoned you that night.'

'But why should anyone—Oh, I see what you're getting at, I think.'

The Superintendent hesitated. He hadn't expected Merle to grasp the implication of his questions quite so rapidly. Now he was faced with a dilemma, either to lie to a sick man, which he preferred to avoid, or to risk over-exciting him. One glance at Merle's bright, intelligent eyes decided him, and he explained as briefly as he could.

'Poor Helen,' Merle said. 'She was a good woman, a good Christian. Why should anyone wish her dead? Her money?

She promised me five thousand for the church, but God knows I wouldn't have wanted it this way. An accident was bad enough, but murder—'

It was a long speech, and had visibly exhausted Merle. A grey tinge came over his face, his eyes closed and he began to breathe shallowly through his mouth. Thorne wondered if he should call the nurse, but he remembered the equipment continuously monitoring the patient's condition and was reassured. And after a couple of minutes Merle appeared to recover.

'Sorry,' he said. 'Sorry.'

'I'm sorry too,' Thorne said. 'We must go. We're tiring you. But there is just one more question. Twelve years ago—'

'No,' said Merle as soon as the Superintendent had completed his explanation. 'I didn't know. We never discussed our private lives, though I think she guessed about me. We talked mostly about books and music and art—and religion, of course.'

'Never about sex—or social problems?'

'Once I recall she said the Church lacked understanding of such matters.' Merle's expression was wry. 'I was scarcely in a position to contradict her. That's all, Superintendent. Perhaps if I'd been in Windfield when she had this—this trouble, she might have turned to me, but I've only been here seven—eight years, as you know. In any case, I doubt it. Helen was a very private person.'

'A very private person.' It was a remark echoed by Mary Band when Thorne telephoned her on his return to Headquarters. But Mary was little more help than Timothy Merle. Helen, she said, had once hinted to her of a serious love-affair, but had implied that it had been part of her London life, not at all connected with Colombury or Windfield. The fact that Helen had been living at South Winds at the time of her pregnancy, Mary dismissed as irrelevant. Helen, she pointed out, had gone to London fairly often, and had travelled elsewhere on behalf of the Galleries. Mary was certain that Helen had never consulted her husband on the subject; even if professional considerations had prevented him mentioning it to his wife while Helen was alive, these would certainly have been overriden by her death—and the manner of it.

And asked what she thought the Draytons' attitude might have been, had Helen told them, she said, 'They're a stuffy pair, Biddy especially. She's very conventional, like her mother, old Muriel. They might have stood by Helen. Their instinct would have been to avoid a scandal at all costs. They'd have been ashamed if it had become general gossip. I hate to think what they're feeling now they're aware the police know.'

'Too bad.' Thorne was not sympathetic.

'George,' Mary said quickly, sensing that Thorne was about to bring the conversation to an end, 'George, may I ask something? This is an old story—twelve years old. What on earth can it have to do with Helen's death?'

'Mary, I haven't an idea,' the Superintendent said truthfully. 'Probably nothing at all.'

It was when he was preparing for bed that night, and somewhat despondently reviewing the events of the day, that Superintendent Thorne realized that Mary Band might possibly have been of greater help to him than he had at first thought. She had reminded him of old Muriel—Muriel Fayne, whose existence, or lack of it, he had practically forgotten.

CHAPTER 19

It was just before six o'clock the next morning when Superintendent Thorne was awakened by the telephone beside
his bed. Jerked from a deep sleep, he instinctively put out
an arm and lifted the receiver as quickly as possible, in an
effort to avoid waking Miranda, sleeping peacefully beside
him.

'Yes,' he said quietly. 'Thorne here.'

'Dick Band. George, I'm speaking from the hospital in
Oxford. I thought you should be told as soon as possible.'

'What is it? Merle?' Forgetful of his wife. Thorne raised
his voice.

'No, no, George. It's Paul Drayton. He's tried to commit
suicide.'

'Tried? He's still alive? How did he do it?'

Beside him Thorne felt Miranda slide out of bed, and
heard her murmur, 'Breakfast.' He nodded vigorously,
propped himself up on an elbow and listened to Dick Band.
Band had a lot to say.

'Drayton's alive, all right. He was damned lucky—or
unlucky, depending on your point of view. He took enough
flurazepam—that's a fairly strong non-barbiturate hypnotic
used as a sleeping pill—to make sure he'd never wake up.
He's had a regular prescription for them from me for months,
and presumably he's been saving them in case he decided
to kill himself. Then he wrote a brief note saying, 'Sorry,
but I cannot go on. Paul,' and went to bed with a bottle of
whisky.

'It should have worked all right, but Peter Drayton had
been to a party in Oxford. He got home about two in the
morning—I suspect about twenty minutes after his father

took his dose. Peter's bedroom's next to his dad's, and as he passed his dad's door he heard what he describes as "a horrid mixture of snores and groans". He was amused for a moment, he says, and went into his room and undressed. But the noise continued. He could hear it clearly through the wall, and it occurred to him that his father might be ill. So he went to see, found the note, woke his mother and phoned me.

'Of course, I guessed what he'd taken, called an ambulance and the hospital immediately, and went over to give him an injection. That kept him going till we got to hospital, where they washed out his stomach and generally gave him a pretty unpleasant time. That's about all I can tell you, George, except that there's no doubt Paul will live.'

For a moment there was silence on the line as Thorne absorbed the news, and took in the possible implications. Then he began to fire questions at the doctor.

'Capsules or tablets?'

'What? Oh, I see. These things come in capsule form.'

'Can I talk to Drayton, interview him?'

'Not at present. He's sleeping, they tell me—quite naturally, now. He's exhausted. A stomach wash-out isn't any fun, you know. But when he wakes, certainly this afternoon, you ought to be able to see him.'

'What happened to his note?'

'I've got it. Peter had knocked it on to the floor when he tried to rouse his father, and luckily I found it. Otherwise, I think they might have tried to claim it was an accident. As you can imagine, Mrs Drayton considers suicide something pretty shameful.'

'If he was making so much noise, why didn't he wake his wife?'

'They sleep in separate rooms, have done so for years evidently, and she's a heavy sleeper. She takes tranquillizers, too.'

'Did either of them—Biddy, Peter—express any surprise at what had happened?'

'Not exactly surprise. Their first reaction seemed to be to want to excuse it, to explain it. Peter said his father had been very much on edge, as he put it, lately, and he'd wondered before if perhaps he wasn't well. That was another reason why he went to investigate last night.'

'And Mrs Drayton? Did she have anything to say?'

'She said Paul was worried about the Galleries, though she was sure his worry wasn't necessary. With Peter's help they'd be able to manage perfectly well, though of course they'd miss Helen.'

'Anything else you think I should know?'

'I don't—believe—so.' Band spoke slowly. 'I'll drop in the suicide note at your Headquarters on my way back to Colombury. If you want me later, phone the surgery and they'll find me.'

'Right. Thanks, Dick. Thanks.'

Thorne put down the receiver and swung his legs over the side of the bed. He sat there, in the red and white striped pyjamas that Miranda had bought for him, and stared straight ahead for a full minute, before he called his office and arranged for a uniformed man from Oxford to be put on guard beside Drayton immediately. Then he telephoned Bill Abbot.

'—Get there as soon as you can, Sergeant, and stay with him, unless some doctor drives you out,' he concluded. 'The important thing is to keep an eye on his visitors. Understand?'

'Yes, sir. I'll be there in half an hour.'

Miranda brought in a tray with tea and buttered toast— weak tea with lemon, as George liked it. He told her what had happened as he ate and drank.

'At least no one was able to suggest it was an accident, thanks to Band,' he said gratefully, his mouth full. 'There've been too many supposed accidents in this case. And it's unlikely to have been a murder attempt. It's all but impossible to persuade someone to swallow a collection of capsules against his will. But why should Paul Drayton try to take his own life?'

It was a rhetorical question, but Miranda suggested an answer. 'Fear,' she said. 'Fear of something worse than death.'

Thorne nodded. 'I'd be interested to know what Drayton considers worse than death,' he said.

Three hours later, Superintendent Thorne wondered if he now had the answer. The letter, addressed to him and marked Personal and Urgent, had arrived at Kidlington in the morning's post. It was not a long letter and, since he had read it several times, he now knew it almost by heart. Still he couldn't bring himself to put it down.

Dear Superintendent Thorne,

By the time you receive this, I shall be dead. I intend to take an overdose of sleeping pills, and not wake up. This will mean the minimum trouble for everyone, because I suspect you believe I caused the death of my sister-in-law, Helen Fayne. I did. I tried to make it appear an accident, but I was not successful. I wanted her dead so that I would own the whole of the Drayton Galleries, and could sell the establishment. Due to unwise investments, I needed the money.

Yours sincerely,
Paul Drayton.

'You couldn't want anything more explicit than that,' said the Chief Constable when Thorne reported all these developments to him an hour later. 'I assume you'll charge Mr Drayton as soon as possible. He had opportunity, means—

Peter Drayton might well be an accessory; we know the boy's dabbled in drugs. And now we've got motive, which Drayton himself has given you in his confession. I don't see any cause for delay, Superintendent. Naturally, we must check the obvious facts, but that should be routine.'

Was it becoming too simple, Thorne wondered, as he drove himself to the hospital. He mulled over the case, concentrating on Paul Drayton and his relationship to the sequence of 'accidents' that had led to Helen Fayne's death.

Drayton could easily have entered South Winds and loosened a stair rod. The Faynes seemed to have no idea of security and the house was always open to family and friends, or for that matter to anyone who was prepared to take a minor risk. The same argument applied to the substitution of the antacid tablets. What was more, if the substituted tablets had been those originally prescribed for Muriel's insomnia, as Band believed. Drayton's chances of acquiring them would have been better than many.

The piece of Esquimo sculpture that had almost fallen on Helen's head, Thorne was inclined to dismiss as a genuine accident, though Drayton could have seized the opportunity to push her under it, only to be thwarted by Timothy Merle. But this would have been a risky business, demanding very rapid thought on Drayton's part. On the other hand, the bolting mare incident had certainly been no accident, and Drayton was supposed to have been in the Galleries that morning; Thorne made a mental note to check if he had left for any length of time.

There remained Helen's final and fatal 'accident'. It was a fair assumption that in the confusion Drayton would have had an opportunity to put something in that last whisky, though he couldn't have foreseen the precise nature of any opportunity that might arise. And where had he got whatever drug it was? The Chief Constable had hinted at Peter as the source, but Thorne couldn't believe that Drayton would have involved his son—unless, he thought wearily, there had been a conspiracy between them.

Then why was he still worried? Was it the note itself? He could recall every word—every stilted word. It was as if Paul Drayton had wanted to make absolutely certain there was no possibility of misunderstanding, so that the case would be closed. Reasonable? The Superintendent shrugged mentally.

He parked his car and went into the hospital, only to meet the doctor in charge of Timothy Merle. The news was encouraging; Merle was gaining strength and had been moved from the ICU to a private ward. Cheered by this, the Superintendent set off to find Paul Drayton who, he reminded himself, was probably responsible for Merle's condition.

A nurse showed Thorne to a small private room at the end of a corridor, where a police constable sat outside the door. Drayton himself looked white and exhausted, and seemed to be asleep. Sergeant Abbot was beside him, but there was no sign of any of the family. Thorne signalled to Abbot to come outside. They walked a short distance away from the constable, so as not to be overheard.

'Any visitors?' Thorne asked.

'Yes, sir. Mrs Drayton, Susan and the two sons. They came this morning while he was still asleep, and went away to lunch. They've been back since; in fact, they've just left. This time Drayton was awake. Susan was in floods of tears, assuring her father that she loved him, they all loved him and asking why he'd been so silly. Mrs Drayton was outwardly far more controlled, but I'm sure she was under great stress. Gavin's gone back to work now. He seemed the least affected. Peter's taken both the women home. He didn't have much to say, but I'd guess he's the one who cares the most.'

'What did Paul have to say?'

'Only, "I'm sorry. I'm sorry," over and over again. Then he started to cry and turned his head away.' Abbot grimaced. 'It was a pretty pathetic exhibition, sir.'

'I dare say,' Thorne said, and thought he could argue that there would be little point in charging Paul Drayton formally until he was fully capable of understanding his situation. 'Have you had any lunch, Sergeant?' he inquired at last.

'Oh yes, sir, thank you. The nurse brought me a tray. Good it was, too.'

Thorne, who had had a couple of dreary sandwiches at his desk, made no response. 'Then I've got some jobs for you. Listen.' He gave Abbot instructions. 'Understand?'

'Yes, sir. I'll do my best.'

'Right. I'll spend a while with Drayton—I can use the uniformed man as a witness—and meet you at Headquarters later in the afternoon. By that time and with any luck we'll have tied up some loose ends.'

Thorne had a word with the constable and together they went into Paul Drayton's room. Paul Drayton lay, eyes closed, breathing gently. The Superintendent took the chair beside the bed, while the constable perched on an uncomfortable stool just inside the door, notebook poised. Thorne waited, allowing Drayton a couple of minutes to adjust to his presence, then he said, quietly but firmly, 'Mr Drayton. I know you're awake, so please stop pretending. I need you to answer some questions.'

Drayton's eyes opened. 'You've got my letter?'

'Yes, Mr Drayton, and in view of its contents I must first warn you that you need not answer any questions, but—'

As the Superintendent uttered the standard formula, Paul Drayton smiled. 'I never expected to hear that,' he said. 'I thought I'd be dead by now.'

'As soon as your state of health permits, Mr Drayton, you'll be taken from here to a police station and charged with causing the death of Mrs Muriel Fayne and . . .'

'No!' The exclamation was involuntary, and an expression of horror passed across Paul Drayton's face. 'Not Muriel. Dear God!' He bit his bottom lip and a thin trickle of blood ran down his chin. He pushed himself up in bed, so that he was sitting. 'It was Helen I killed. Helen, not Muriel. No one killed Muriel. Her death was an accident. Why—why should anyone kill Muriel? Helen . . .' He seemed unable to continue.

Thorne decided to help him. 'You put a drug in Helen Fayne's drink at the Clutton-Greys' party?'

'Yes, that's right, Inspector—Superintendent, whatever you call yourself.' Drayton was clearly relieved at the change of subject.

'What kind of drug?'

Paul hesitated momentarily. 'Amphetamines—you know, pep pills,' he said finally. 'They made her—'

'Where did you get them? From Peter?'

'Yes. No. Well, indirectly. Some years ago Peter got in a spot of trouble, and I kept some of his stuff.'

'You mean you were contemplating killing your sister-in-law some years ago, Mr Drayton? Your financial situation was satisfactory then, surely.'

'I didn't . . . I wasn't . . . I . . .'

'All right, Mr Drayton,' Thorne said soothingly. 'Don't get upset. Let's come forward to the present. The use of this drug wasn't the first recent attempt you'd made to dispose of Miss Fayne, was it? Tell me about the dart.'

'The dart? I—I don't know how you found out about that. Well, it belonged to my grandson, Jeremy. I took it from his toy cupboard. I stood behind the hedge and waited for Helen—she nearly always rode along that lane—and I threw the dart into the horse's behind after she'd passed me. I hoped the animal would bolt, and throw her, and do the job for me. But it didn't work out like that.'

'Meanwhile Peter was at the Galleries, and would give you an alibi by swearing you were there too?'

'No, no! Why do you keep on about Peter? He knew nothing about it, any of it. It was me. I killed Helen!' Drayton's voice rose. 'It was my fault, all my fault. No one else's. Oh God, why don't you accept what I say? I've had enough!'

Before Thorne could stop him, Drayton put out a hand and pressed the red emergency bell. Nurses came running.

CHAPTER 20

When Superintendent George Thorne returned to his Head-quarters at Kidlington he was informed that Peter Drayton was waiting for him in one of the interview rooms, with a uniformed constable to keep him company. Sergeant Abbot had not yet returned, but he had phoned in a message which was on Thorne's desk. The Superintendent took his time. He glanced through his in-tray, made a few telephone calls, and finally went along to the room where Peter Drayton was growing steadily more and more irate.

On Thorne's arrival, he exploded. 'What the hell is this all about? You know my father tried to—to kill himself. You know he's in hospital. And yet you—'

'Your father will live, as you're perfectly well aware,' Thorne said brutally. He pointed to a chair facing the light. 'Sit down, Drayton! There!'

Peter Drayton did as he was told. Thorne took a seat behind the small table, which was bare except for a telephone and a sheet of clean blotting-paper, and the constable moved his chair to one side and produced a notebook and ballpoint, ready to take notes on his knee. It was an uncompromising, uncomfortable room, not furnished or equipped to put an interviewee at ease. Peter Drayton, now his anger had subsided, was clearly disturbed by his circumstances. He wriggled in his chair, fidgeted with the collar of his shirt, and several times wet dry lips.

'Now,' Thorne said. 'What do you know about your father's finances?'

The question astounded Peter, who shook his head in disbelief at its apparent irrelevance. 'Why should I answer questions about our private affairs? Why can't I have a solicitor—'

'Please, Mr Drayton,' Thorne said mildly. 'You're only helping us with our inquiries. Try to cooperate.'

Peter hesitated. Finally, 'Oh, all right,' he said. 'My father's finances. I don't know much. He's comfortably off, I'd say.'

'Have there been any recent signs that he needed to economize?'

'Not that I know of. Why don't you ask him? He's ordered a new car, and he and my mother are going on a Caribbean cruise next January.'

'Thank you,' said the Superintendent. Peter Drayton's comments confirmed information he had been able to glean on the phone from other sources, and of course contradicted Paul Drayton's own assertions. Abruptly Thorne changed the subject.

'Do you remember the afternoon your grandmother died?'

'Yes, of course.'

'Where were you?'

'Me? At the Galleries.'

'Mrs Band couldn't find you immediately when she came in that day. Where were you? And where were the others?'

'Aunt Helen was calling on the Slinters. Dad had gone home. He wasn't feeling well; he thought it was something he'd eaten. And I—I *was* there, in the office at the back. I remember Mrs Band was a bit peeved I hadn't heard the shop bell. Actually, I was making a long-distance phone call, something I'm not meant to do from the Galleries without permission.'

There was a back service door to the building, Thorne reflected, which gave straight on to the office corridor. He continued, 'So you can't give any details of your father's movements. He could have gone to south Winds on his way home, for instance?'

'I suppose so, yes. But why should he?'

'Was your mother at home that afternoon?'

'No. She'd gone to Oxford to do some shopping. I remember that because Aunt Helen told me to phone her about Gran, and I only got Dad.'

For a minute there was silence. Thorne contemplated the blotting-paper on the table in front of him, apparently seeking inspiration from it. Peter Drayton continued to fidget nervously. At last he could stand the pause no longer.

'Superintendent, what is all this about?' he demanded. 'My brother's at work, and so is Andrew Hill. I'm needed at home.'

'I shan't keep you longer than is necessary,' Thorne said. 'Tell me, have you now, or have you recently, had in your possession any hallucinogens—hallucinatory drugs, like LSD for example?'

'No—o.' Peter Drayton stared at the Superintendent.

'Are you absolutely certain? Would you prefer to alter that reply? Because I must tell you frankly that I don't believe you. Lying to the police is a serious offence.'

'Okay.' Drayton was beginning to sweat. 'You hop from one subject to another, and you confuse me. I did have a few mescaline capsules. I—I'm not sure where . . . Oh, all right, I've still got them, in my room, hidden under the carpet where there's a sort of crack in the floorboards.'

'Where your father might have found them?'

'Are you crazy? Dad would be furious if he knew I still

had any. He made me swear after . . . after . . .'

'After you last had trouble with the police over drugs.' Thorne completed the sentence. 'How many capsules are left?'

'I don't know. Honestly, I don't. I only took one. That was enough. The result terrified me. I thought I was going mad.'

'Try to think how many.'

'I don't know, I say. I can't for the life of me think why I kept them . . .'

Peter Drayton's words poured out. Thorne nodded encouragement, thankful that he now knew how Helen Fayne had met her death. But Peter Drayton, he realized, could be an accessory to murder. He must give him a warning before he went any further.

Peter Drayton's face paled at the formal words. 'But why?' he demanded. 'What are you charging me with?'

'Possession of drugs would be sufficient to start with,' the Superintendent said. 'But for now just listen and answer my questions. Okay?'

Then he said, 'Mr Drayton, you should know that your father has confessed to causing the death of your aunt, Helen Fayne, by administering to her a drug at a party at the home of Sir Reginald Clutton-Grey shortly before she crashed her car. The drug in question was an hallucinogen. We have evidence of that. Its effects caused her to drive into that stone wall.'

'No! I don't believe it!' Peter Drayton swallowed hard. 'Not Dad. Never. He'd never have hurt Aunt Helen. Why should he? He depended on her for the Galleries and they —they were very close.' Peter Drayton hesitated, but said no more.

Thorne said, 'Mr Drayton, your father has admitted his action. He tried to kill himself because he thought the police had begun to suspect him. Now, I must ask you, did you supply him with the means—a capsule of mescaline? If you did—'

'No! I did not.' Peter Drayton made a helpless gesture. 'Superintendent, this is becoming a nightmare. I don't—I can't believe my father tried to kill Aunt Helen.'

'Not only tried, but succeeded.'

Peter Drayton said, 'Sometimes I've wondered—perhaps I shouldn't say this—but I've wondered whether Father wasn't half in love with her.'

'Why did you think that?' Thorne asked sharply.

'The way he looked at her occasionally. Probably I was just being silly, but—'

The telephone on the table rang loudly. Thorne picked up the receiver and listened. The speaker on the other end of the line talked for two or three minutes. The Superintendent said nothing but 'yes' and 'no' and finally, 'Thanks, Sergeant Abbot.' Then he replaced the receiver and turned back to Peter Drayton.

'Your father also admits to having attempted to cause Helen Fayne's death on at least one previous occasion, by throwing a dart at her horse and making it bolt. Mr Drayton, very few people know why Vain Glory, normally a placid beast, suddenly bolted that Saturday morning—and they are all above suspicion, except the individual who threw the dart.'

'You mean, how did Dad know about the dart? That's one thing that's easily explained. He guessed. We all did. It wasn't hard,' Peter Drayton replied at once. 'You kept on asking about the darts that Gavin gave Jeremy. Of course you had some reason. I remember trying to take the mickey out of you, and actually suggesting you thought someone had thrown a dart at poor Aunt Helen's car. It didn't take long for us to realize that wasn't quite as silly as it sounded, if it was the horse, not the car. We all talked about it. Mother did say I was being foolish, but anyway that's how Dad got the idea.'

'I see,' said Thorne. 'Apart from your parents, did you mention this theory to anyone else?'

'Yes, I said so. We all talked about it—Gavin and the Hills and—I can't remember. Is it important, Superintendent? I'm sorry, but it was just a joke originally—an example of police stupidity, if you like.'

'It also happens to be the truth. We've known that for some time. Your Aunt Helen knew it too. She found the dart.'

Peter Drayton was not stupid; his mind was quick when he cared to use it. 'Mescaline and Jeremy's dart,' he said thoughtfully. 'They add up to—to someone in the family or very close to it. I see that. But it doesn't have to be Dad.' He pushed back his chair and stood up. 'I'm going to talk to him.'

'No, Mr Drayton, you're not.' The Superintendent had also risen. 'You're staying here—in a cell. As you say, your father doesn't have to be guilty. You also had the means, the opportunity, and a motive. Your share of your aunt's money would give you more freedom to do what you want than you've ever had before. And, of course, your grandmother had to die first, so that South Winds would be part of Helen Fayne's estate.'

The Superintendent was busy during the next couple of hours. Peter Drayton was not charged. That, as Thorne said in his hearing as he was being led away, could wait till next morning and, to Thorne's surprise, Peter, though he protested, made no further demand to see a lawyer and appeared resigned to a night in the cells.

But a search warrant for the Draytons' house had to be obtained before members of the Drugs Squad could search the place, and Thorne had to brief the officers in question. He also had to confer with Sergeant Abbot on his return to Kidlington. And finally he had to consult the Chief Constable. Throughout these chores he felt that sense of urgency which often assailed him towards the end of a case, when he had identified the villain, but still hadn't sufficient evidence to convince his Chief or the DPP.

At long last, however, the Superintendent was able to set off with Abbot, again to the hospital. Doctors or no doctors, he was now determined to extract the truth from Paul Drayton. He was convinced that Drayton's confession was spurious, and in his opinion there was only one reason why Drayton should have 'confessed', and been prepared to take his own life to prove his guilt.

Once seated beside Paul Drayton's bed, with Abbot perched on the uncomfortable stool, Superintendent Thorne wasted no time. He said, 'Mr Drayton, perhaps I should tell you that your son, Peter, is in custody at the moment, helping us with our inquiries. He has admitted having an hallucinatory drug in his possession, which itself is an offence. And of course you say you gave a drug to Helen Fayne with intent to cause her death.'

'Peter knows nothing about it!' Drayton exclaimed violently. 'I mean, he didn't know I'd taken it.'

'So he maintains,' Thorne said. 'Where did you find it?'

There was a pause, then Drayton said, 'I shan't answer that. Why—why should I incriminate Peter?'

'All right,' said Thorne. 'Then tell me why you tried to kill the Reverend Timothy Merle. Was it because he had followed Helen Fayne down the Clutton-Greys' driveway, and could perhaps give evidence about her behaviour— evidence that would suggest she was hallucinating?'

'I—er—yes. And he wouldn't let things alone. He wanted further inquiries into Helen's death. I was afraid.'

'So what did you do?'

'I ran him down in the lane. I drove straight at him. Then I went on in to Colombury to the Galleries. I'd arranged it so that Sergeant Court would be there to give me an alibi.'

'Clever of you,' Thorne said. 'How did you lure the vicar to the lane at that time of night?'

'I phoned him,' Drayton said after a moment's hesitation.

'*You* phoned him? What did you say?'

'I—I can't remember exactly.'

'Of course you can't,' Thorne agreed, suddenly amicable. 'You can't because you're telling lies, Mr Drayton.' Abruptly he changed the subject. 'What about the corrugated cardboard?'

Paul Drayton's mouth opened and shut. He had no answer to the Superintendent's question. And he knew he had been trapped. He turned his back on Thorne, and buried his face in the pillow. 'It was all my fault, my fault,' he said. 'Go away.'

'No, Mr Drayton,' said Thorne. 'If you won't tell me, I'll tell you. Mr Merle did receive a phone call—an urgent call —to go to a well-known local farming family called Gotobed, chosen because his obvious route to them would be down that little-frequented lane. It was, of course, a hoax. When he cycled down the lane his killer was waiting for him, and ran him down. You, incidentally, were on your way to the Galleries by this time in response to another hoax, having left your wife to do what she planned to do.'

There was a lengthy silence . . .

Then Paul Drayton turned slowly around to face the Superintendent. Tears stained his face, but he looked drained of all emotion. 'If only I had died,' he said.

'It would have made no difference, Mr Drayton. The police don't give up so readily. Nor do they accept confessions without supporting evidence—in spite of what you may have heard or read. So you wouldn't have saved her. Come on, now, Mr Drayton,' he added more gently. 'It's too late for lies. You must realize that. You'll only do more damage to your family. Won't you tell me the truth?'

'What do you want to know?' Paul Drayton said at last.

Thorne heaved a sign of relief. 'First, your relationship with Helen Fayne,' he said. 'You were lovers, weren't you?'

'Yes. Years ago,' Paul Drayton said wearily. 'I loved her very much. She was a wonderful person. She was a bit like a witch to look at, but she was clever in so many ways, and kind and much too good for me. She ought to have married. She'd have made someone a splendid wife. Instead, she . . .' Drayton's voice trailed off.

'Had an *affaire* with her brother-in-law,' Thorne prompted, 'and conceived his child.'

Drayton suddenly threw off his weariness. 'It's not for you to judge her—or me,' he said angrily.

'No, perhaps not. I'm sorry,' Thorne said. 'Go on.'

'I wanted her to go away with me and have the baby, though she was really too old to bear a first child, but she refused to break up my marriage because of Biddy and my children. Susan was only fifteen at the time, and I'd always been close to the kids.' Paul Drayton sighed heavily. 'Then when Helen came back from London, after the—the operation, she refused to—to make love any more, and we became literally just good friends.'

'Did your wife know?'

'Not at the time. We were always very careful.'

'But she found out, didn't she?' Thorne said. 'About you and her sister—and the child? That's when she decided to kill Helen, making it look like an accident. And she didn't care if she didn't succeed at once, because that way she could enjoy seeing Helen hurt or scared. Yes, Mr Drayton, you *are* right. You do deserve some of the blame, but not all, or even the major part of it—certainly not enough to pay for it with your life.'

CHAPTER 21

Some weeks later the Thornes invited the Bands to dinner.
Bridget Drayton had been charged with murder, by administering a noxious substance to her sister, Helen Fayne, with
intent to cause her death. At the preliminary hearing before
the magistrates' court, bail had been refused, and she was
in prison, awaiting trial. The police were still collecting
detailed evidence for the prosecution—it was painstak-
ing work—but Detective-Superintendent Thorne was
satisfied that he had unearthed his villain and produced a
reasonably watertight case against her; judgement was not
his business.

Dick and Mary Band were naturally eager to hear the
inside story from Thorne. And, as Miranda said, they owed
the Bands a meal. This evening the four of them were having
a before-dinner drink in the Thornes' sitting-room, and
the Superintendent had already outlined the course of his
inquiries.

'I can understand how you decided it must be a member
of the family or someone very close—everything pointed
that way—but I still can't imagine how you decided it was
Biddy, rather than Paul or one of the young,' Dick Band
said as Thorne stopped speaking to sip his whisky.

'Partly character and partly luck,' Thorne said. 'I found
it hard to conceive of Peter or Gavin or Susan deliberately
killing their aunt for the sake of the money they'd get, though
you could argue that all three of them had reason to want
it. What's more, if Gavin had planned to kill her, I believe
he'd have set about the job in a simple, businesslike fashion,
and certainly not through a series of hit-or-miss accidents.
He's too clever for that. As for Susan—'

'You can't seriously have considered Susan,' Mary objected.

'Why not? She was desperate to get a bigger house—and many murders have been done for less. But in my opinion she's just not clever enough. She wouldn't have known about the drugs. No. Of the three, Peter was the most obvious suspect.'

'You did arrest him,' Miranda said. 'That must have given him a scare.'

'He deserved that for keeping the mescaline. Anyway, I only held him so that he couldn't warn his mother, either on purpose or unwittingly.'

'I can't think why she left the tube in place for you to find,' Mary said.

'Ah, I wondered about that,' replied Thorne. 'But if Peter had missed it, he might have become suspicious, and the last thing Bridget Drayton wanted was to draw any attention to the wretched drug. Anyway, I'm thankful she didn't destroy it.'

Dick Band said, 'You haven't yet told us why it couldn't have been Peter or Paul.'

'It could, on the surface,' said Thorne. 'But again it was a matter of opinion and impressions. Paul hasn't got the guts, to be blunt. He's a nice chap, but weak.' Thorne shrugged; he didn't want to sound like an amateur psychiatrist. 'Peter's much the same kind of fellow, though maybe a bit tougher underneath his facile exterior. Biddy, however, struck me as being definitely tough and determined. Everyone claimed she was a selfish woman, like her mother, and used to getting her own way.

'But what first made me consider her twice—if I can put it like that—was the speed and efficiency with which she dealt with young Jeremy after his birthday party. Somehow, it was out of character. I think I'd have expected her to let the other women cope, but of course she guessed what the boy had done, and she was clever enough to cover it up. Luckily the initial emergency treatment for food poisoning and an overdose are much the same.' Thorne looked at Band, who nodded, then went on. 'The trouble, from my point of view, was that she had no apparent motive at all.'

'So that's where the luck came in?' Mary said. 'Mrs Slinter's gossip, that turned out to be a great deal more than gossip. But the events it related to were long ago—twelve years ago, George. Why on earth should Biddy wait till now?'

'That's one of the questions we're still trying to answer, and Bridget Drayton's not cooperating; ten to one her defence will raise the point. Personally, I feel certain she only found out recently. I believe Muriel told her, though how Muriel knew I don't know. That's a loose end, though I don't think it's an important one. Maybe Helen had morning sickness or something, and Muriel guessed. Maybe Muriel saw a letter or heard a phone call. Helen would have had to make arrangements for her abortion, and she was living with Muriel at the time, remember.'

'Then I'll rephrase the question,' Mary said. 'Why did Muriel wait till now to tell Biddy?'

'I think I can answer that, though it could be hard to prove. There's evidence that Biddy and Muriel had a serious row, some of which Mrs Ferguson overhead. Mrs F. thought the quarrel was connected with who would inherit South Winds when Muriel died. She caught the words ". . . selfish bitch . . ." and ". . . no wonder Paul and . . ." and ". . . child . . .". But, if it was the vital conversation, it must have shattered Biddy, who had accepted over the years that her sister was clever, but singularly unattractive. If we're right, it's what led to the tragedy. Biddy killed Muriel—'

'Muriel?' Dick Band interrupted.

'Yes, though I doubt if we could ever prove it. Muriel

had to be got out of the way before Biddy could start playing cat-and-mouse with Helen. First, because Muriel knew— and was the only one except Paul to know—that Biddy had good cause to hate Helen. Secondly, because, with Helen dead, Biddy would be expected to give Muriel a home.'

'That last point seems pretty weak,' Mary commented.

'As I said,' replied Thorne, 'she was a selfish woman.'

Thorne looked up as Miranda returned from the kitchen to the sitting-room. She had disappeared to her domestic chores several minutes before; she had already heard the details, and was no longer as curious as the Bands.

'I've got to interrupt,' she said. 'Dinner's ready.'

But neither the excellent homemade soup, nor the breaded veal cutlets served with sauté potatoes and baby carrots and mangetout peas could keep the conversation away from Helen Fayne and her family.

'What will happen to them now?' Mary wondered.

'Well,' said Thorne, 'I suppose the young will inherit Helen's money. They had nothing to do with her death. Susan won't want South Winds any more—I hear Andrew Hill is leaving Coriston and looking for a job at the other end of the UK—so they'll sell it to Clutton-Grey for a good price, though not, I suspect, the price he once offered Helen. Gavin will set up his computer business. As for Peter—I don't know.'

'I think that in the end Peter will decide to stand by his father,' Miranda said. 'From what you've told me, George, he's fond of Paul, and Paul's going to need help. Eventually, I imagine they'll sell the Drayton Galleries, and move away.'

'And what about Biddy? What's likely to happen to her?' Dick Band asked.

'That's not my business, Dick,' said George Thorne quickly, 'but in my personal opinion she was a cruel woman, and if she'd not been caught now I've got a strong suspicion her husband would have been next on her list.'

There was a sudden wave of disquiet in the room. With Thorne's help, Miranda collected the dishes and took them through to the kitchen. She returned with a raspberry and apple pie. The Superintendent opened another bottle of wine.

'At least one good thing's come out of this unhappy business,' Miranda said as she passed the cream. 'Though Timothy Merle asked that his family shouldn't be told about his accident, the Bishop thought it his duty to keep them informed. The brothers have been reconciled at last.'

'Let's have a toast,' Thorne said. 'To Dick and Mary Band, without whose intervention there would probably never have been an investigation, and to Merle, who was hurt through my incompetence. He provided the catalyst for the case. If it hadn't been for him . . .' The Superintendent raised his glass. 'To you, to him—and to justice,' he said.